Enid Blyton

The
Brer Rabbit
book

Enid Blyton

The Brer Rabbit book

EGMONT

Enid Blyton

EGMONT
We bring stories to life

Originally published in Great Britain in 1948 by Latimer House
as *Enid Blyton's Brer Rabbit Book*
This edition published 2015 by Dean, an imprint of Egmont UK Limited,
The Yellow Building, 1 Nicholas Road
London W11 4AN

ENID BLYTON ® Copyright © 2015 Hodder & Stoughton Ltd
Illustrations © Hodder & Stoughton Ltd

Illustrated by Grace Lodge

Set ISBN 978 0 6035 7152 7
Book ISBN 978 0 6035 7231 9

www.egmont.co.uk

A CIP catalogue record for this title is available from the British Library

Printed in the United Kingdom

61340/1

FSC
MIX
Paper
FSC® C018306

Egmont is passionate about helping to preserve the world's remaining ancient forests.
We only use paper from legal and sustainable forest sources.

This book is made from paper certified by the Forest Stewardship Council® (FSC®),
an organisation dedicated to promoting responsible management of forest resources.

For more information on the FSC, please visit www.fsc.org. To learn more about
Egmont's sustainable paper policy, please visit www.egmont.co.uk/ethical

CONTENTS

Brer Rabbit's Pond

AT THE BACK of Brer Rabbit's house was a round pond. Sometimes, when it got very dirty with leaves falling into it, Brer Rabbit cleaned it out.

One time he cleaned it out beautifully, and then he stood and sighed by the edge of his empty pond.

"If only the rain would come and fill it!" he groaned to himself. "If the rain doesn't come I'll have to fill my big watering-can fifty times and carry it from the tap to the pond!"

Well, the rain didn't come. The sun shone out, and the sky was as blue as forget-me-nots. Not a rain-cloud was to be seen!

"It's no good!" said Brer Rabbit at last. "I'll have to fill the pond myself." So he picked up his big watering-can and filled it at the tap by the side of his house.

He dragged it to the pond and emptied the water in—slishy-sloshy, slishy-sloshy! It made a lovely noise. Brer Terrapin came by, and looked over the wall when he heard the noise.

"My!" he said to Brer Rabbit, "that's a fine game you're having this morning! It's fun to play with water like that. Let me have a turn."

"You can't drag my big watering-can along, old slow-coach!" said Brer Rabbit. But Brer Terrapin soon showed him that he could! He balanced the big can on his back and walked slowly to the pond. He stood with his back to the pond and jerked the can. It poured all the water out at once.

"My, but it's heavy!" panted Brer Terrapin. "I guess you've got a hard job this morning, Brer Rabbit. Why don't you get your friends to come along and help you?"

"Huh! As if Brer Fox and Brer Wolf would fill my pond for me!" said Brer Rabbit.

"You let me manage things for you," said Brer Terrapin with a sly grin. "You let me manage things, Brer Rabbit. You've always been a good friend to me, and if you'll let me have a swim in your pond now and again, I'll just see if I can't get you a bit of help this morning!"

"All right, Brer Terrapin, you try," said Brer Rabbit, and he watched Brer Terrapin crawling out of his gate.

Well, Brer Terrapin, he went down the road, and soon he met Brer Fox.

"Heyo, old shellyback, where have you been this long time?" said Brer Fox.

"Oh, I've just come from Brer Rabbit's," said Brer Terrapin. "And my, he gave me such a treat! He let me help him pour water into his pond! It went slishy-sloshy, slishy-sloshy into the empty pond, a real treat to see it! It's fun to play with water, isn't it, Brer Fox? But it's no use *you* going along to Brer Rabbit's, for I don't suppose he'll give you a treat like that. It's only because I'm a friend of his."

"Well, I'm a friend of his too!" said Brer Fox. "Haven't I known him for years and years? My, I guess we've done more things together than any other creatures in the world. If I want to pour water into his pond, I just *know* he'd let me!"

"All right, you go and see, Brer Fox," said Brer Terrapin, putting his head inside his shell to grin to himself. "You go and see!"

So Brer Fox went along to Brer Rabbit's, and he soon heard Brer Rabbit singing, "Hi ho! Hi ho!" and he heard the sound of water splashing merrily into the pond.

"Heyo, Brer Rabbit!" yelled Brer Fox. "You seem to be mighty busy this morning. That's a fine job you're doing."

"Oh, a mighty fine job!" said Brer Rabbit, winking to himself. "A job that everyone would like to do, Brer Fox. I just gave Brer Terrapin a turn at it, because he's a very old friend of mine, and I like giving him a treat."

"Well, I'm an old friend of yours too," said Brer Fox. "You let me have a turn as well, Brer Rabbit. I don't like Brer Terrapin going around saying he's the only friend of yours that helps you with your pond. You let me have a turn too."

"Why, Brer Fox, I'd be pleased to," said Brer Rabbit. "Yes, yes, you have a turn—have two turns—have ten turns if you want to! I'm not one to be selfish. No—if my friends want a share in my pleasures, they are welcome to them. You take the can, Brer Fox, and have a good time!"

So Brer Fox dragged the heavy can to and fro a good many times, whilst Brer Rabbit sat on the warm sunny wall and smoked his pipe and talked.

Now it wasn't long before Brer Bear and Brer Wolf came along and looked over the wall too.

"Heyo, Brer Rabbit," said Brer Bear. "We've just met Brer Terrapin, and he's been a-boasting and a-bragging that you've let him fill up your pond because he's such an old friend of yours. And he said he was mighty certain you wouldn't give anyone else that treat—and here we see Brer Fox playing with the water too!"

"Oh, Brer Bear," said Brer Rabbit politely, "that's too bad of Brer Terrapin to go around saying I won't give any of my friends but him a chance to play with my pond. Brer Fox, he came along and said just the same thing—and I'm giving him a treat too! If you want to join in, you just say the word. I'm not the man to stop anyone having a good time!"

Well, by this time Brer Fox was nearly worn out with carrying the heavy can. So he spoke up at once.

"And I'm not the man to be selfish either. I'll let Brer Bear and Brer Wolf have a turn now. That's only fair!"

So Brer Wolf and Brer Bear came in at the gate and set to work to fill the can and empty the water into the pond. My, but it was nearly full now! It only needed about four more cans and it would overflow.

Cousin Wildcat looked over the wall and grinned. Brer Rabbit hopped off to the garden-seat, for he didn't trust Cousin Wildcat's claws.

"Heyo, Brer Rabbit," said Cousin Wildcat. "I just heard from Brer Terrapin that you've got Brer Fox and Brer Wolf and Brer Bear doing all your hard work for you. Ah, you're a smart one, Brer Rabbit, no doubt about that! But you don't catch me coming along and carrying your heavy cans for you all morning long. No—my brains are as good as yours *any* day, Brer Rabbit!"

Brer Fox, Brer Wolf, and Brer Bear stood and stared in surprise. Then they turned their eyes on Brer Rabbit, who began to feel mighty uncomfortable. But he put a bold face on it and spoke up well.

"Brer Fox! Brer Wolf! Brer Bear! Are you going to stand there, and let Cousin Wildcat make out I've tricked you, when all you've been doing is to have a treat? You go for him right now, and make him say he's sorry!"

So Brer Fox, Brer Wolf, and Brer Bear jumped over the wall and chased Cousin Wildcat right into the middle of the wood. He fled up a tree and laughed at them. "Go and ask Brer Terrapin!" he cried. "Maybe you'll believe *him*!"

But when the three of them hunted for Brer Terrapin, he was nowhere to be found! He was having a fine swim in Brer Rabbit's nice full pond—and every now and again he would come up to the top and wink his eye at Brer Rabbit. Then down he'd go to the bottom—ker-blinkety-blunk!

Brer Fox and the White Plums

IT HAPPENED ONE MORNING that Brer Rabbit was going through the woods, and he ran bang into old Brer Fox. Brer Fox took hold of Brer Rabbit and looked at him.

"I feel mighty hungry, Brer Rabbit," said Brer Fox.

"Huh, Brer Fox," said Brer Rabbit, trying to wriggle away, "I don't feel hungry myself because I've just been eating a whole lot of white plums." And then Brer Rabbit smacked his lips together and licked his mouth as if he could still taste something nice.

"Brer Rabbit, what in the name of goodness are white plums?" said Brer Fox, astonished, "and how is it I've never seen any?"

"I don't know why you've never seen any," said Brer Rabbit. "Some folks see straight, some see crooked, some see one thing and some see another. I saw those white plums, and more than that, I ate them all up! I ate all that were on one tree, but I expect there are a lot more round about."

Old Brer Fox's mouth began to water.

"Come on, Brer Rabbit, come on!" he said. "Show me where those white plums grow!"

Brer Rabbit hung back as if he didn't want to take Brer Fox. Brer Fox dragged him forward. "Come on, Brer Rabbit, come on!"

But still Brer Rabbit hung back. Then he said, "Hoo, Brer Fox! You want to get me in the middle of the wood all alone and do something to me. You want to take me out there and scare me."

Old Brer Fox, he held up his hands and cried, "I declare to goodness, Brer Rabbit, I wouldn't think of such a thing.

Whatever makes you think that? Come on, Brer Rabbit, and let's go and get those white plums."

"Hoo, Brer Fox, you play so many tricks on folks that I'm afraid to go anywhere alone with you," said Brer Rabbit.

"I won't scare you or do you any harm, Brer Rabbit," promised Brer Fox. So they set out for the middle of the woods, and Brer Rabbit brought Brer Fox to a wild walnut tree. The walnuts were as green as could be, but in the bright sunshine they shone pale and white. The tree was loaded down with unripe nuts. Brer Fox looked astonished.

"Are those white plums?" he said. "It's funny I didn't know that before."

Old Brer Rabbit, he scratched himself and said, "Those are the plums. They may not be as ripe as those I had for my breakfast, but those are white plums as sure as anything. There are red plums, and purple plums, and yellow plums, but these plums are white ones."

"How can I get them?" said Brer Fox.

"You'll have to do as I did, Brer Fox," said Brer Rabbit.

"What's that?" asked Brer Fox.

"You'll have to climb up for them, Brer Fox."

"How can I climb a tree like that?" said Brer Fox, looking up the tall, straight trunk in dismay.

"Oh, grab with your hands, hold tight with your legs and I'll push you behind," said Brer Rabbit.

Well, Brer Fox began to climb, and Brer Rabbit, he began to push till, sure enough, Brer Fox got to where he could grab up and catch the lowest branch of the tree. He heaved himself up and there he was! He climbed on up, he did, till he came to where he could reach a green walnut. He picked it and put it into his mouth whole. He chewed it hard—and then, bless gracious, if Brer Fox didn't forget all his manners! The fruit was so bitter and so hard that Brer Fox nearly fell out of the tree.

He shouted "Ow!" and spat the walnut out of his mouth as

if it was poison, and he made such a face that Brer Rabbit had to have a fit of coughing to hide his grins and giggles.

"You'd better come down, Brer Fox, if the white plums aren't ripe," he shouted up at last. "Come down and we'll go somewhere else."

Brer Fox started down the tree, and he got along well enough till he came to the lowest branch again. When he got there he stopped. He didn't see how he was going to get down the long trunk. He had no claws to cling by, like Cousin Wildcat, and he hadn't much leg either, to hold on with.

Brer Rabbit kept on shouting, "Come on down!" and Brer Fox kept trying to think how to get down.

"Oh, do come on, Brer Fox," said Brer Rabbit. "I pushed you up, didn't I, and if I was anywhere near you I'd push you down too! Come on!"

Brer Fox sat clinging to the lowest bough and looked mighty scared. He wasn't used to climbing trees. By and by Brer Rabbit stood a little way off from the tree and said, "If you'll jump out this way, Brer Fox, I'll catch you."

Brer Fox looked down and he looked all round, and he still looked mighty scared. Brer Rabbit came a little bit closer and shouted, "Hop right down here, Brer Fox, and I'll catch you."

Well, he kept on like this till by and by Brer Fox made up his mind to jump into Brer Rabbit's arms—and what's more, Brer Fox meant to get hold of old Brer Rabbit, too, and tell him what he thought of his white plums! But he didn't say that—no, he kept quiet, and just thought of a few things he'd say to old Brer Rabbit.

So Brer Fox jumped straight at Brer Rabbit, but just as he jumped Brer Rabbit hopped out of the way, yelling, "Ow! Ow! Excuse me, Brer Fox! I trod on a thorn! Excuse me, Brer Fox! I trod on a thorn!"

And old Brer Fox, he hit the ground like a sack of potatoes, and all his breath was knocked out of him. When he got up he counted all his legs and his tail to see if they were still there, and then he sat down and licked himself hard.

As for Brer Rabbit, he was nowhere to be seen; but I guess it will be a long time before Brer Fox goes looking for white plums again!

The Wonderful Tar-Baby

ONE DAY, after Brer Rabbit had tricked Brer Fox with the calamus root, Brer Fox went to work and got some tar and mixed it with turpentine, and made a thing he called a tar-baby.

The tar-baby was like a little black man, and looked very funny. Brer Fox took his tar-baby, gave it a hat and set it by the lane. Then he hid himself in some bushes to see what would happen.

He didn't have to wait long, because by and by Brer Rabbit came along, galloping down the road, lippity, clippity, just as saucy as a jay-bird. Brer Fox lay low. Brer Rabbit came prancing along till he spied the tar-baby, and then he sat up on his hind legs in astonishment. The tar-baby sat there, and Brer Fox, he lay low.

"Morning!" said Brer Rabbit to the tar-baby. "Nice weather today!

The tar-baby said nothing, and Brer Fox, he lay low.

"How are you feeling this fine day?" said Brer Rabbit.

Brer Fox winked to himself and lay low, and the tar-baby said nothing at all.

"What's the matter with you? Are you deaf?" said Brer Rabbit. "Cos if you are, I can shout louder."

The tar-baby stayed still, and Brer Fox, he lay low. Brer Rabbit got angry.

"You're stuck-up, that's what you are!" said Brer Rabbit "and I'm going to cure you, that's what I'm going to do!"

Brer Fox sort of chuckled inside himself, but the tar-baby said nothing.

"I'm going to teach you how to talk to nice people if it's my last act!" said Brer Rabbit. "Now just you listen to me—if you don't take off your hat and say, 'How do you do?' to me, I'm a-going to hit you into the middle of next week!"

The tar-baby stayed still, and Bear Fox, he lay low.

Brer Rabbit kept on telling the tar-baby to be polite, and the tar-baby kept on saying nothing, so presently Brer Rabbit drew back his fist and hit the tar-baby on the side of the head—blip!

And that's just where he made a mistake. His fist stuck in the tar-baby, and he couldn't pull it loose. The tar held him. But the tar-baby stayed still, and Brer Fox, he lay low.

"If you don't let me loose, I'll hit you again," said Brer Rabbit, and with that he hit out with his other hand—and that stuck too! The tar-baby said nothing, and Brer Fox, he lay low.

"Turn me loose, or I'll kick the stuffing out of you!" said Brer Rabbit, but the tar-baby, she said nothing at all. She just held on, and then Brer Rabbit kicked out at her with all his might—and his feet stuck too. Brer Fox still lay low.

Then Brer Rabbit squealed out that if the tar-baby didn't turn him loose, he would butt her so hard she would go lop-sided.

And then he butted her—blip! And his head stuck too. Then Brer Fox, he strolled out of the bushes, looking as innocent as a day-old lamb.

"How do you do, Brer Rabbit?" said Brer Fox. "You look sort of stuck-up this morning!" And then Brer Fox rolled on the ground and laughed and laughed till he couldn't laugh any more.

"I expect you'll have dinner with me *this* time, Brer Rabbit!" he said. "I've got some calamus root for you, and I'm not going to take any excuse. You've just got to come to dinner with me this time!"

Old Brer Fox rolled on the ground again and laughed till he cried. "Well, I expect I've got you this time, Brer Rabbit," he said. "Maybe I haven't, but I think I have! You've been running round here cheeking me for a mighty long time, but I expect you won't do it any more. You've been dancing about and bouncing around until you think you're the biggest person here. And you are always somewhere that you've got no business to be," said Brer Fox. "Who asked you to come and talk to this tar-baby? And who stuck you up where you are? Nobody in the world!"

Brer Rabbit said nothing. He just stayed stuck and thought hard.

"You just threw yourself at that tar-baby without waiting to be invited," said Brer Fox. "And there you are, and there you'll stay till I fix up a wood-pile and set it alight, because I'm going to cook you this day, sure enough!" said Brer Fox.

Then Brer Rabbit talked mighty humbly:

"I don't care what you do with me, Brer Fox," he said, "so long as you don't fling me in that brier-bush. Cook me, Brer Fox, but don't fling me in that brier-bush!"

"It's too much trouble to make a fire," said Brer Fox. "I think I'll have to hang you."

"Hang me as high as you please, Brer Fox," said Brer Rabbit, "but for goodness' sake don't fling me in that brier-bush!"

"I haven't got any string," said Brer Fox, "so I expect I'll have to drown you."

"Drown me as deep as you please, Brer Fox," said Brer Rabbit, "but don't fling me in that brier-bush!"

"There's no water near," said Brer Fox, "so I expect I'll have to skin you."

"Skin me all you like, Brer Fox," said Brer Rabbit, "but please, please don't fling me in that brier-bush!"

Well, Brer Fox wanted to hurt Brer Rabbit just as much as ever he could, so he thought he *would* fling him into the prickly brier-bush! He caught him by the hind legs and slung him right in the middle of the brier-bush—blim!

There was a great to-do when Brer Rabbit hit the bush, and Brer Fox sort of hung around to see what would happen. By and by he heard somebody calling him, and away up the hill he saw Brer Rabbit sitting cross-legged on a log, combing the tar out of his fur with a wood-chip.

Then Brer Fox knew he had been badly tricked. Of course, Brer Rabbit had to be saucy, and he shouted out:

"I was bred and born in a brier-bush, Brer Fox—bred and born in a brier-bush!" And with that he skipped off just as lively as a cat on hot bricks!

Brer Rabbit Gets a Riding-Horse

BRER RABBIT STAYED in his house till the tar from the tar-baby rubbed off his fur, but it wasn't many days before he was galloping up and down the place the same as ever, and perhaps a little cheekier than before.

Well, the tale about how Brer Rabbit got stuck in the tar-baby soon got round, and everyone laughed to hear it. Miss Meadows and the girls, who were great friends of Brer Rabbit, heard the tale too—and when Brer Rabbit paid them a visit, Miss Meadows asked him about it, and the girls began to giggle.

But Brer Rabbit sat up just as cool as a cucumber, and let them giggle.

By and by he crossed his legs and winked his eye slowly. Then he said:

"Ladies, Brer Fox was my daddy's riding-horse for thirty years; maybe more, but thirty years anyhow!" Then he bowed politely, put on his hat, and marched off as stiff and straight as a walking-stick.

Well, the next day Brer Fox went calling on Miss Meadows and the girls, and as soon as he began to laugh about Brer Rabbit being stuck up in the tar-baby, Miss Meadows told him what Brer Rabbit had said.

"Brer Rabbit says you were his daddy's riding-horse for thirty years," she said. "Well, well, fancy you being ridden by a rabbit, Brer Fox!"

Brer Fox snapped his jaws and looked mighty angry to hear such a thing. He stood up to go, and said:

"Ladies, just wait till I get hold of Brer Rabbit! I'll make him chew up his words, sure enough!" And with that off Brer Fox marched.

And when he got to the main road he shook the dew off his tail and made straight for Brer Rabbit's house. When he got there, Brer Rabbit was expecting him, and the door was shut fast.

Brer Fox knocked—blim, blam! Nobody answered. Brer Fox knocked again—blim, blam! Still nobody answered. Then he knocked a third time—blim, blam!

Brer Rabbit called out in a mighty weak voice: "Is that you, Brer Fox? I want you to run and fetch the doctor. The dish of parsley I ate this morning is making me feel bad. Do, please, Brer Fox, ran quickly!" said Brer Rabbit.

"I've come for you," said Brer Fox. "There's going to be a party up at Miss Meadows'. All the girls will be there, and I promised that I'd fetch you. The girls said it wouldn't be a proper party unless you were there, and they made me fetch you."

"I'm too sick to come," said Brer Rabbit.

"You're all right!" said Brer Fox. "A party will put you right, Brer Rabbit. It's what you're needing."

"I'm not needing anything," said Brer Rabbit in a weak voice. "You just go away, Brer Fox. You make me feel worse."

"You're bound to feel bad if you go and shut yourself up on a fine day like this," said Brer Fox. "Come along with me, and smell what a fine day it is."

"The day smells all right," said Brer Rabbit. "It's you that doesn't smell so good to me, Brer Fox."

"The girls will be mighty sorry if I go back without you," said Brer Fox.

"I can't walk, I'm so weak," said Brer Rabbit.

"Well, I'll carry you," said Brer Fox.

"How?" said Brer Rabbit.

"In my arms," said Brer Fox.

"You'll drop me," said Brer Rabbit.

"I won't," said Brer Fox.

15

"Well," said Brer Rabbit, after a bit, "I'll come with you if you'll carry me on your back, Brer Fox."

"That's all right with me," said Brer Fox at once. "Come on, Brer Rabbit, or the party will be over."

"I can't ride on your back unless I have a saddle to sit on," said Brer Rabbit. "I'd be slipping off all the time."

"I'll get you a saddle," said Brer Fox.

"It's no good me sitting in a saddle unless I've some reins to hold on by," said Brer Rabbit.

"Well, I'll get a bridle," said Brer Fox.

"I won't ride you unless you wear blinkers," said Brer Rabbit. "If you don't wear blinkers, Brer Fox, you'll be shying at the tree-stumps along the road, and I'll fall off."

"I'll get some blinkers," said Brer Fox.

"You get all those things and I'll go to the party," said Brer Rabbit.

"Now, see here, Brer Rabbit," said Brer Fox, "I'll just carry you to the lane outside Miss Meadows' house, but you must get down and walk the rest of the way."

"That suits me all right," said Brer Rabbit, and then Brer Fox ran to fetch the saddle, the reins, and the blinkers.

Now Brer Rabbit knew quite well that Brer Fox meant to take him to Miss Meadows' and make him tell them it wasn't true that Brer Fox had been his daddy's riding-horse, and he made up his mind to trick Brer Fox. By the time he had combed his hair and twisted up his whiskers along came Brer Fox with the saddle and bridle on, looking as smart as a circus pony. He trotted up to the door and stood pawing the ground and champing the bit in his mouth like a proper horse. Brer Rabbit got on his back and they ambled off.

Brer Fox couldn't see him behind him, because he was wearing blinkers over his eyes, but by and by he felt Brer Rabbit lift up one of his feet.

"What are you doing, Brer Rabbit?" he said.

"Just pulling up my sock, Brer Fox, just pulling up my sock," said Brer Rabbit.

By and by Brer Rabbit lifted up the other foot.

"What are you doing now, Brer Rabbit?" said Brer Fox.

"Just scratching my toe, Brer Fox, just scratching my toe," said Brer Rabbit.

But all the time, gracious goodness, Brer Rabbit was cutting on sharp spurs, and when they got close to Miss Meadows', where Brer Rabbit should have got off, Brer Rabbit slapped the spurs into Brer Fox's skin, and my word, didn't Brer Fox gallop along! Every time he slowed down, Brer Rabbit just stuck those spurs into him again, and Brer Fox let out a yell and galloped on at top speed.

When they got to the house, Miss Meadows and the girls were sitting outside on the verandah, and instead of stopping at the gate, Brer Rabbit rode right through it, and up to the horse-rack. He jumped off Brer Fox, threw the reins over the horse-rack, and ambled into the house grinning all over his face.

He shook hands with everyone, and sat down to smoke a big cigar. Then he took the cigar out of his mouth, puffed out a cloud of smoke, and said:

"Ladies, didn't I tell you Brer Fox was the riding-horse for our family? He's not so fast now as he was, but I dare say he'll get better after I've ridden him for a month or two!"

And then Brer Rabbit grinned, and the girls giggled, and Miss Meadows said what a fine pony Brer Fox was. Brer Fox was hitched tightly to the horse-rack and couldn't loose himself.

"You just wait till you ride me home, Brer Rabbit!" said Brer Fox, gritting his teeth. "You just wait!"

17

Brer Rabbit is in a Hole

WELL, YOU REMEMBER that old Brer Rabbit had ridden Brer Fox up to Miss Meadows' house, saddle and bridle and all, and hitched him to the post there. Everyone laughed and talked and sang and then at last the time came to go home.

"Well, it's time I was a-going," said Brer Rabbit. "My horse will be pawing the ground to bits, soon, if I don't go out to him. Good-bye, Miss Meadows, good-bye, girls, and thanks for a wonderful party. It was real kind of Brer Fox to fetch me along!"

Brer Rabbit went to the horse-rack, where Brer Fox was tied, walking as though he owned the whole world. He jumped on to Brer Fox's back and rode off, waving his hat to the girls.

Brer Fox didn't say anything at all. He just tore off and kept his mouth shut, and Brer Rabbit sort of felt there was trouble coming. So he held on to the reins tightly and waited to see what old Brer Fox was going to do.

Brer Fox ambled on till he got into the long lane, out of sight of Miss Meadows' house, and then he just went wild! He ripped and he roared, he snorted and cavorted, he reared and he bucked!

He was trying to fling Brer Rabbit off his back. But he might just as well have tried to fling off his own shadow. Every time he humped himself up, Brer Rabbit slapped the spurs into him, and there they went, up and down, up and down! Brer Fox fairly tore up the ground, and he jumped so high and he jumped so fast that he nearly snatched his own tail off!

They kept on like this, till by and by Brer Fox lay down on the ground and rolled over. This sort of unsettled Brer Rabbit, and he fell off—but by the time Brer Fox was up on his feet again, Brer Rabbit was rushing through the wood faster than a racehorse!

Brer Fox set out after him, and he went so fast that he caught him up, and Brer Rabbit only just had time to get into a hollow tree. The hole he shot in by was too small for Brer Fox, and he had to lie down and rest and get his breath again.

Well, while Brer Fox was lying there, all out of breath, Brer Buzzard came flapping along, and saw Brer Fox stretched out on the ground. Brer Buzzard flew down beside him and looked at him. Then he shook his wings sadly, put his head on one side and said:

"Brer Fox is dead, and I'm so sorry."

"No, I'm not dead," said Brer Fox. "I've got old Brer Rabbit shut up in here, in this hollow tree, and I'm going to get him this time, if it takes till Christmas!"

Then, after some more talking, Brer Fox made a bargain with Brer Buzzard, and Brer Buzzard promised to watch the hole and keep Brer Rabbit there whilst Brer Fox went to fetch his axe. So Brer Fox galloped off, and Brer Buzzard took up his stand by the hole.

By and by, when everything was still, Brer Rabbit sort of scrambled round close to the hole and shouted out:

"Brer Fox! Oh, Brer Fox!"

Brer Fox had gone, and nobody said anything. Then Brer Rabbit squealed out as if he were mad.

"You needn't talk unless you want to, Brer Fox," he said. "I know you're there, and I don't care if you are! I just want to tell you that I wish old Brer Turkey Buzzard was here!"

Then Brer Buzzard tried to talk like Brer Fox. "What do you want with Brer Buzzard?" he said.

"Oh, nothing in particular, except that there's the fattest grey squirrel in here that ever I saw," said Brer Rabbit, "and if Brer Turkey Buzzard was around he'd be mighty glad to get him!"

"How could Brer Buzzard get him?" said Brer Buzzard.

"Well, there's a little hole round on the other side of the

tree," said Brer Rabbit, "and if Brer Buzzard was here so\ that he could stand just there, I'd drive out that squirrel to him."

"Drive him out," said Brer Buzzard, hopping round to the other side of the tree, "drive him out, and I'll see that Brer Buzzard gets him!"

Then Brer Rabbit kicked up such a noise, just as if he were really driving out a squirrel, and when he heard old Brer Buzzard going round the tree to get the squirrel, Brer Rabbit dashed out of the hole and raced for home!

Well, when Brer Buzzard saw Brer Rabbit rushing off, he felt mighty lonesome, but he had promised Brer Fox that he'd stay, and he thought he would hang round and see what Brer Fox would say when he found Brer Rabbit was gone. He didn't have to wait long, because by and by Brer Fox came galloping through the woods with his axe on his shoulder.

"How's Brer Rabbit getting on, Brer Buzzard?" said Brer Fox.

"Oh, he's in there," said Brer Buzzard. "He's mighty still, though. I expect he's taking a nap."

"Then I'm just in time to wake him up," said Brer Fox. And with that he threw off his coat and grabbed his axe. He brought it down on the tree-trunk—pow! And every time he struck the tree with the axe—pow!—Brer Buzzard did a little dance and shouted out:

"Oh, he's in there, Brer Fox. He's in there, sure enough!"

And every time a chip flew off, Brer Buzzard would jump and dodge and shout, "He's in there, Brer Fox. I just heard him. He's in there, sure enough!"

And Brer Fox, he lammed away at that hollow tree, till by and by, after he had almost cut the tree through he stopped to get his breath—and he saw Brer Buzzard laughing at him behind his back. And straight away, Brer Fox knew something was up. But Brer Buzzard, he kept on shouting:

"He's in there, Brer Fox. He's in there! I've just seen him!"

Then Brer Fox pretended that he was peeping into the tree, and he said: "Come here, Brer Buzzard, and see if this is Brer Rabbit's foot hanging down!"

And Brer Buzzard came stepping up and stuck his head in at the hole; and no sooner had he done that, than Brer Fox grabbed him. Brer Buzzard scrambled round and flapped his wings, but it was no use. Brer Fox had got him fast.

Then Brer Buzzard squealed out loudly, "You let me alone, Brer Fox. Turn me loose! Brer Rabbit will get out! You've nearly cut the tree through. A few more cuts and you'll have Brer Rabbit!"

"I'm nearer to you, Brer Buzzard, than I'll be to Brer Rabbit today!" said Brer Fox. "What did you trick me for?"

"Let me alone, Brer Fox," said Brer Buzzard. "My old woman's waiting for me. Brer Rabbit's in there!"

"There's a bunch of his fur on that blackberry bush," said Brer Fox. "That's the way he went, Brer Buzzard."

Then Brer Buzzard told Brer Fox all about it. "And Brer Rabbit's the greatest rascal that ever lived!" he said.

"That's neither here nor there, Brer Buzzard," said Brer Fox. "I left you to watch this hole and I left Brer Rabbit in there. I come back and I find you at the hole and Brer Rabbit gone. I'm going to make you pay for it. I'm going to fling you on a wood-pile and burn you up!"

"If you fling me on the fire, Brer Fox, I'll fly away!" said Brer Buzzard.

"Well, then, I'll settle you right now!" said Brer Fox, and he grabbed Brer Buzzard by the tail to dash him to the ground—but it was just about the time of year when the tail feathers of buzzards drop out, and Brer Buzzard sailed up into the air like a balloon, leaving a few feathers in Brer Fox's hand!

"You've given me a good start, Brer Fox!" shouted Brer Buzzard, and Brer Fox had to sit there and watch him fly out of sight!

Poor Sis Cow!

AFTER BRER RABBIT had escaped out of the hollow tree, he went skipping along home, just as saucy as a jay-bird. He went galloping along, he did, but he felt mighty tired out and stiff in his joints, and he was dying for something to drink.

By and by, when he was almost home, he spied old Miss Cow feeding in a field, and he thought he'd see if she would give him a drink. Brer Rabbit had a feeling that Miss Cow wouldn't give him any milk at all because she had said no often enough, even when Brer Rabbit's old woman was sick. But never mind—Brer Rabbit was going to try again!

He danced up to the fence and called out loudly to Miss Cow: "Howdy, Sis Cow!"

"Why, howdy, Brer Rabbit!" said Miss Cow.

"How are you these days?" said Brer Rabbit.

"Oh, so-so, just so-so," said Miss Cow. "How's yourself, Brer Rabbit?"

"Oh, I'm just so-so myself, Sis Cow," said Brer Rabbit. "Not too bad but not too grand either!"

"How are your folks?" said Miss Cow.

"Just middling, Sis Cow," said Brer Rabbit. "How's Brer Bull getting on?"

"Bellowing as usual," said Miss Cow.

Then Brer Rabbit looked at a tree near by. "There are some mighty nice apples up this tree, Sis Cow," said Brer Rabbit, "and I'd like mighty well to have some!"

"How are you going to get them?" asked Miss Cow.

"Well, I thought I might ask you to butt your head against the tree and shake some down for me," said Brer Rabbit.

Well, Miss Cow thought she might as well do it as not,

so she marched up to the apple-tree. She hit it a rap with her horns—blam!

But those apples were as green as grass, and not one dropped off the tree! Then Miss Cow butted the tree again—blim! Not an apple dropped. Then Miss Cow backed away a little, took a run, and knocked the apple-tree hard—blip! No apples dropped, not even a tiny one.

Then Miss Cow backed off a little further, hoisted her tail over her back, and ran at the tree again—kerblam! And she came so fast, and she came so hard that one of her horns went right into the trunk, and there she was, stuck fast! She couldn't go forwards and she couldn't go backwards.

This was exactly what Brer Rabbit was waiting for, and he no sooner saw old Miss Cow all stuck up than he began to grin and rub his hands in joy.

"Come and help me out, Brer Rabbit," said Miss Cow.

"I can't climb, Sis Cow," said Brer Rabbit, "but I'll run and tell Brer Bull to help you."

And with that Brer Rabbit set out for his home, and it wasn't long before he came back again with his old woman and all his children—and every single one of his family was carrying a pail! The big ones had big pails and the little ones had little pails.

They all surrounded Miss Cow, and they milked her till she hadn't a drop of milk left. The big ones got their pails full, and the little ones got their pails full too. When they had got enough Brer Rabbit said:

"I wish you mighty well, Sis Cow. I'm afraid you'll have to camp out all night, but it doesn't look like rain, so maybe you'll be all right."

Then off he went home, he and all his family carrying their pails so as not to spill a drop.

Well, Miss Cow, she stood there, she did, and tried to think how to get loose. She pulled and she jerked at her horn, but it was jammed too tightly in the tree to come out. But at last, when she jerked it mighty hard, just before day, she got it loose.

She grazed round in the field a bit, for she was hungry. Old Miss Cow thought that Brer Rabbit would soon be hopping along that way to see how she was getting on, and she thought she would lay a trap for him.

"I'll stick my horn back into the hole just before Brer Rabbit comes along," thought Miss Cow. "Then he'll think I'm still stuck fast, and he'll come up to me—and won't I kick out at him and won't I chase him round the field and stick my horn into him! I'll teach you to trick old Sis Cow, Brer Rabbit, so I will!"

Well, just about sunrise what did old Miss Cow do but march up to the apple-tree and stick her horn back into the hole, just as she had planned. But she didn't do it quite soon enough! Brer Rabbit had come hopping quietly along, and he was in a corner of the field, watching her.

Brer Rabbit was surprised to see Sis Cow loose—and even more surprised to see her sticking her horn back into the tree!

"Heyo !" he said to himself. " What's all this going on? Just wait a minute, and I'll find out!"

He crept out of the field and went back down the road a little way. By and by he came along—lippitty-clippitty-lippitty-clippitty—galloping down the main road.

"Morning, Sis Cow," said Brer Rabbit. "How do you feel this morning?"

"Poorly, Brer Rabbit, poorly," said Miss Cow. "I haven't had any rest all night. I can't get my horn out of the tree. But if you'll come and catch hold of my tail, Brer Rabbit, I reckon maybe I can get my horn out!"

Then Brer Rabbit came a little closer, but he didn't come *too* close!

"I think I'm near enough, Sis Cow," said Brer Rabbit. "I'm a mighty little man, and if I come any nearer you might trample on me. You do the pulling out, Sis Cow, and I'll do the shouting!"

Then Miss Cow pulled out her horn in a rage and tore after Brer Rabbit. Down the road they went, Brer Rabbit with his ears laid back, and Miss Cow with her head down and her tail up. Brer Rabbit ran fast and by and by he darted into a brier-patch. By the time Miss Cow came along he had his head sticking out, and his eyes looked as big as saucers.

"Heyo, Sis Cow!" said Brer Rabbit, not looking a bit like himself. "Where are you going?"

"Hallo, Brer Big-Eyes," said Miss Cow. "Have you seen Brer Rabbit go by?"

"He's just this minute passed," said Brer Rabbit, "and he looked mighty sick, Sis Cow."

When she heard that, Miss Cow tore off down the road as if the dogs were after her—and Brer Rabbit, he just lay down there in the brier-patch and rolled and laughed till his sides hurt him. He simply *had* to laugh. Fox after him, Buzzard after him, Cow after him—and they hadn't caught him yet!

Mr. Lion's Soup

ONCE MR. LION put on his tall hat, reached for his stick, and set out to have his dinner at Brer Possum's Hotel. He felt hungry, and he made up his mind to have a really good dinner.

"I'll have oxtail soup!" said Mr. Lion to himself, as he walked along, swishing off the daisy-heads with his stick, which was very wrong of him. "Yes, oxtail soup, rich and thick and tasty. Aha!"

He reached Brer Possum's Hotel and went up the steps. As soon as the hall-porter saw him he rushed to greet him, for Mr. Lion was a very honoured customer. If people didn't pay attention to him, he got very angry, so the waiters flocked round him, and Brer Possum himself helped him off with his coat.

"Give me the best table," said Mr. Lion in his growly voice. So they gave him the best table, and he sat down, tucking his tail neatly under the chair.

"What will you have to eat, Mr. Lion, sir?" asked Brer Possum, beckoning to Brer Hare, Brer Raccoon, and Brer Hedgehog, all waiters.

"Bring me some oxtail soup," said Mr. Lion in a very commanding sort of voice.

Brer Possum flew to tell the cook to make some oxtail soup. Very soon it was ready. It was poured into a silver tureen, and taken to Mr. Lion's table. He sniffed at it as it was poured into his soup-plate.

"It smells good," he said.

"It *is* good," said Brer Hare, the waiter, waiting for Mr. Lion to begin tasting it. But Mr. Lion didn't. He sat there, and didn't taste it at all.

"What's the matter, Mr. Lion?" asked Brer Hare, seeing a

frown beginning to come on Mr. Lion's great forehead.

"I can't eat this soup," said Mr. Lion.

"Oh, sir!" said Brer Hare, alarmed. "I hope it's good! Is it too hot?"

"I don't know," said Mr. Lion. "I can't eat it."

Brer Hare flew to get Brer Raccoon, and took him over to Mr. Lion's table. Brer Raccoon bowed anxiously before the great Mr. Lion.

"What is the matter, sir? "he asked.

"I can't eat this *soup*!" said Mr. Lion.

"Has it too much pepper in it?" asked Brer Raccoon anxiously. "The cook does sometimes use the pepper-pot too much."

"I don't know," said Mr. Lion. "All I know is that I can't eat my soup!"

Brer Raccoon flew to get Brer Hedgehog. "He says he can't eat his soup," said Brer Raccoon, nodding his head backwards towards Mr. Lion. "What are we to do?"

"I'd better go and see if it's got too much onion in," said Brer Hedgehog, dropping his napkin in his hurry, and tripping over his prickles. "He doesn't like onion."

So he scampered to Mr. Lion's table and bowed low. "Mr. Lion, sir," he said, "I'm sorry to hear about this. Has your soup got too much onion in?"

"I don't know," said Mr. Lion, in a rage. "I tell you I can't eat my soup!"

"Well, I'll fetch Brer Possum," said poor Brer Hedgehog, in a panic, and he shot off to get the master of the hotel. Brer Possum was horrified to hear that Mr. Lion couldn't eat his soup, and he hurried at once to his table.

"I'm sorry the soup is not to your liking," he said. "Do tell me what is wrong, Mr. Lion. You didn't find a fly in it, I hope, or a caterpillar?"

"No," growled Mr. Lion, looking fiercer than ever.

"Well, has it too much salt in it?" asked Brer Possum, shivering with fear, for he knew Mr. Lion's habits when he was displeased.

"I don't know," said Mr. Lion. "All I say is—I can't—eat—my—SOUP!"

"Well, sir, I'll fetch the cook who made it," said Brer Possum, trembling. "It was Brer Raccoon's old woman who made it. Just wait a minute and I'll get her."

In a few moments Brer Raccoon's wife came shuffling along, looking very scared indeed, twisting up the corners of her apron, and looking ready to cry, for she was very much afraid of Mr. Lion.

"Good morning, sir," she said, dropping a curtsey. "I hear you can't eat the soup I made."

"No, I can't possibly," said Mr. Lion gloomily.

"But, sir, it's made of the very best ox-tail that ever was," said Brer Raccoon's old woman eagerly. "And I didn't put much onion into it, and only a little pepper and salt, and it was nice and hot when it left my kitchen."

"All the same, I can't eat it," said Mr. Lion, still more gloomily.

"Well, let me take it away and bring you another kind," said Mrs. Raccoon, and she stretched out her paw to take the plate. But Mr. Lion shouted at her so loudly, and showed his teeth so fiercely, that she backed away in alarm.

"Leave my soup!" shouted Mr. Lion. "I want to eat it, but I can't. I HAVEN'T GOT A SPOON!"

Well, well, well! Just to think of that! Brer Raccoon got him a spoon, and Brer Hedgehog gave him one, and Brer Possum and Brer Hare did too. They were all so pleased to find that nothing was really wrong with the soup. As for silly old Mr. Lion, he only had himself to blame if the soup was cold!

Oh, Brer Rabbit!

ONE DAY, after Brer Fox had been doing all he could to catch Brer Rabbit, and Brer Rabbit had been doing all he could to stop him, Brer Fox said to himself that he'd play a trick on Brer Rabbit.

And no sooner had he said the words than Brer Rabbit came lolloping up the road looking as plump and as fat as a blackbird in spring.

"Half a minute, Brer Rabbit!" said Brer Fox.

"Can't stop, Brer Fox," said Brer Rabbit, going a bit faster.

"I want to have a talk with you, Brer Rabbit," said Brer Fox.

"All right, Brer Fox but you'd better shout to me from where you are. I'm not coming any nearer," said Brer Rabbit.

"I saw Brer Bear yesterday," said Brer Fox, "and he said he was shocked because you and I don't make friends and live in peace, and I told him that I'd see about it."

Then Brer Rabbit scratched one of his ears with his hind foot sort of doubtfully, and said, "Right you are, Brer Fox. Suppose you drop round tomorrow and take dinner with me. We don't have anything fancy at our house, but I expect my old woman and the children can scramble round and get something to fill you up."

"Fine!" said Brer Fox.

"Then I'll see you tomorrow," said Brer Rabbit.

Next day Brer Rabbit and old Miss Rabbit got up early, before day, and got some cabbages and corn and sparrow-grass, and fixed up a splendid dinner.

By and by one of the little rabbits, playing out in the backyard, came running in, shouting, "Oh, Ma! Oh, Ma! I saw Mr. Fox a-coming!"

And then Brer Rabbit, he took his children by their ears and made them sit down, and then he and Miss Rabbit waited about for Brer Fox. And they kept on waiting, but Brer Fox didn't come.

After a while Brer Rabbit went to the door and peeped out— and what do you think he saw? Why, sticking out from behind the corner was the tip-end of Brer Fox's tail!

"So Brer Fox is a-hiding there, ready to jump out on us!" said Brer Rabbit, with a grin. He shot indoors and sat down. He put his paws behind his ears and began to sing:

"I won't go out this morning,
I don't like getting shocks,
'Cos where you see a tail,
You're sure to find a fox!"

Then Brer Rabbit and old Miss Rabbit and all the little rabbits grinned at one another and ate up the dinner as fast as they could.

Next day Brer Fox sent Brer Mink to say that he was sorry he hadn't come to dinner the day before, but he was too ill to come, and please would Brer Rabbit come and take dinner with him! Brer Rabbit said yes, he would.

So by and by, when the sun was high in the sky, Brer Rabbit brushed his fur well, and wandered off down to Brer Fox's house. When he got there he heard somebody groaning, and he peeped in at the door and there he saw Brer Fox sitting up in a rocking-chair all wrapped up in flannel, and looking mighty weak.

Brer Rabbit looked all round, but he didn't see any dinner. The dish-pan was on the table, and close by was a large carving knife.

"Looks as if you're going to have chicken for dinner, Brer Fox," said Brer Rabbit.

"Yes, Brer Rabbit, all nice and fresh and tender," said Brer Fox.

Then Brer Rabbit pulled at his whiskers and said, "You haven't got any calamus root, have you, Brer Fox? You know I just simply can't eat chicken unless it's seasoned with calamus root."

And with that Brer Rabbit shot out of the door and dodged into some bushes. He sat there, hidden, waiting and watching to see what Brer Fox would do.

He hadn't watched very long before he saw Brer Fox fling off his flannel and creep out of the house, ready to pounce on Brer Rabbit when he came back.

"So that's his little game!" grinned Brer Rabbit to himself. He sat a little longer, and then he shouted loudly:

"Oh, Brer Fox! I'll just put the calamus root out here on this tree-stump! You'd better come and get it whilst it's fresh!"

And then Brer Rabbit galloped off home. So Brer Fox didn't catch him after all—and he's not going to either!

Brer Rabbit Lays in his Winter Stores

NOW ONE TIME the winter set in very early, and the creatures couldn't seem to find enough to eat. Brer Fox got as thin as a broom-handle, and Brer Rabbit was just a bag of bones.

One day they met in the road and began to talk.

"Bad times, Brer Rabbit, bad times," said Brer Fox.

"You've nothing to grumble at, Brer Fox," said Brer Rabbit. "You've got a horse and cart, and I've got nothing except my old wheelbarrow!"

"What's the use of a horse and cart?" said Brer Fox. "You just tell me that, Brer Rabbit—what's the use of a horse and cart when you've got nothing to carry in it? Why, I used to go to the town and bring back my cart full of food—but now the horse is lazing in the field and the cart is lying idle in the shed."

"That's bad," said Brer Rabbit. "Why don't you sell your horse and cart, Brer Fox, and buy food with the money? I'm surprised that a clever man like you hasn't thought of that before."

Well, Brer Fox thought it over and he reckoned it was a mighty good idea. Having a horse and cart wouldn't help him if he was dying of hunger!

"Well," said Brer Fox, "that's a good idea, Brer Rabbit—but if I go to town and sell my horse and cart to buy food, I'll have no cart to bring it home in and no horse to pull it! So I'd be no better off than before!"

"Well, Brer Fox," said Brer Rabbit, "I don't mind giving you a hand over this. I'll lend you my wheelbarrow to bring your shopping home in. We can put the wheelbarrow in the cart when we set out, and after you've sold your horse and cart, you can buy food with the money and put it into my barrow. I'll take turn and turn about in wheeling it home!"

"That's mighty good of you, Brer Rabbit," said Brer Fox. "I'll do that. Meet me at the corner of the road tomorrow morning and we'll set off for town."

So the next morning the two of them set off in the cart. Brer Fox clucked to his horse and they galloped into the town. Pretty soon Brer Fox had sold the horse and cart and had money to jingle in his pockets.

My, the food he bought! It just made old Brer Rabbit's mouth water, so it did! A sack of rice, a sack of corn, a sack of coffee, a sack of turnips—it was a wonder it all went into the barrow!

"You take a turn at wheeling the barrow first, Brer Rabbit," said Brer Fox. "My arms ache from driving the horse."

Brer Rabbit lifted the handles of the barrow. My, but it was heavy! Brer Rabbit puffed and panted and Brer Fox grinned to see him. Brer Fox walked fast and Brer Rabbit couldn't keep up with him. He did his best, but Brer Fox always seemed to manage to keep so far ahead that Brer Rabbit couldn't shout loudly enough to him to make him hear.

Well, at last Brer Rabbit's arms were aching so much that he had to put the barrow down.

"Heyo, Brer Fox!" he yelled. "You come along back here! It's your turn now!"

Brer Fox went skipping along in front and didn't so much as turn his head.

"Brer Fox! BRER FOX! You come along back here!" yelled Brer Rabbit. "I'm not going to wheel your food all the way home. You give me my share for helping you, and I'll take it and go."

Brer Fox heard that all right. He turned round and grinned at Brer Rabbit.

"The food's mine!" he shouted. "I may give you a handful of rice, Brer Rabbit, but that's all you'll get! Aha! Some one else can play tricks, as well as you!"

Brer Rabbit thought mighty hard, he did. Then he shouted to Brer Fox.

"All right, Brer Fox. Just give me my handful of rice and I'll be off. But you might pop into Brer Bear's house just over there and ask him for a little bag to put my rice in. I can't carry it in my paws very well."

So Brer Fox, grinning to himself and feeling mighty pleased

with things, bopped along to Brer Bear's house and borrowed the smallest bag he could.

Now as soon as Brer Fox was out of sight, Brer Rabbit took hold of the sack of rice and pulled it out of the barrow. He hid it under a bush, but before he left it there he put his hand in at the top and got a handful of rice grains out. He ran back to the barrow and then set off in the opposite direction, dropping the rice as he went. Then back he went to the barrow again and sat down by it, pretending to cry.

By and by Brer Fox came back with a small bag, and when he got there he saw Brer Rabbit crying. My, but he was boo-hooing!

"In the name of goodness, Brer Rabbit, what's the matter?" said Brer Fox.

"Matter enough, matter enough!" said Brer Rabbit. "I wish you'd stayed here instead of going off, Brer Fox."

"What's up then, Brer Rabbit?"

"Oh, a man came, Brer Fox, and stole your lovely bag of rice!" sobbed Brer Rabbit. "I ran after him but he went too fast for me."

"Which way did he go, Brer Rabbit?"

"There's the way he went, Brer Fox, there's where he dropped the rice out of the sack as he ran. If you're quick, Brer Fox, you'll catch him!"

Brer Fox dropped the bag he carried and tore off, hoping to catch the man that Brer Rabbit spoke of. He was hardly out of sight when Brer Rabbit caught hold of the bag of coffee and carried that away to the bush and hid it too. He put his hand into the top of the sack, took out some coffee beans, ran back to the barrow, and then set off in the other direction, dropping the beans as he went. It looked just as if some one had run there with a sack, dropping beans out of it as he ran!

After a while, back came Brer Fox, a-puffing and a-panting. He hadn't seen any man at all. Brer Rabbit shouted to him.

"You haven't come a minute too soon, Brer Fox! While you were gone another man came and carried off the coffee. See, that's the way he went, Brer Fox, and if you're quick, you'll catch him!"

Well, Brer Fox set off again as fast as he could, and he ran and ran, but he didn't see any man at all. Whilst he was gone Brer Rabbit carried off the sack of corn, and sprinkled some grains in the opposite direction again. Then Brer Fox came back, shouting that he hadn't seen any one—and Brer Rabbit yelled to him to say that another man had been and had carried off the corn.

Well, this suddenly seemed mighty queer to Brer Fox—all these men coming by that way, in a lonely place, and stealing out of his barrow. He wondered if maybe Brer Rabbit was up to one of his tricks, so when he ran off, pretending to chase the man again, he didn't go very far, but turned round and crept back to see what Brer Rabbit was doing.

And he was just in time to see Brer Rabbit pulling at the sack of turnips in his barrow! Well, Brer Fox was mighty tired with running hither and thither and backwards and forwards, but he felt so mad when he saw what Brer Rabbit was up to that he dashed up to him and shouted at him.

"What are you going to do with that sack of turnips?" he yelled.

Brer Rabbit put the sack down and looked very upset. He looked at Brer Fox as if he felt mighty sorry for folks who asked such foolish questions. He shook his head, he did, and said:

"Well, well, well! Who'd have thought Brer Fox would have come yelling at me like this, when any one would guess I was just a-carrying it off to save for him, so's no man could steal it?"

But this sort of talk didn't deceive Brer Fox, and he snarled so fiercely that Brer Rabbit thought it would be better to run— and run he did, with Brer Fox at his tail, between the trees. And at last Brer Rabbit came to a hollow tree and in he went!

Well, old Brer Buzzard was a-sailing round in the air, and Brer Fox called to him.

"Just you watch this hole for me, Brer Buzzard," said Brer Fox. "I'm a-going to fetch some fire to smoke old Brer Rabbit out!"

Well, Brer Fox set off, and Brer Buzzard settled down beside the hole—and after a bit Brer Rabbit sang out, "I've got the better of you, Brer Buzzard! I surely have!"

"How's that, Brer Rabbit?" said Brer Buzzard.

"Because I can see you and you can't see me!" said Brer Rabbit, in his most cheeky voice.

With that Brer Buzzard stuck his head in the hole of the tree and looked up to see Brer Rabbit, and no sooner did he do this than Brer Rabbit flung a handful of sand down into his eyes.

Poor Brer Buzzard! He blinked and he winked but he couldn't get the sand out—so down to the stream he flew to wash his eyes. And whilst he was gone Brer Rabbit came down out of the hollow tree, and raced back to the barrow.

It wasn't long before he had taken the sacks of corn, rice, and coffee out from under the bush where he had hidden them, popped them into the barrow with the sack of turnips, and trundled away merrily to his home.

And my, didn't Brer Fox shake his fist when he passed by Brer Rabbit's house the next day and smelt fried ricecakes and fresh coffee! Ah, it's no use trying to trick Brer Rabbit!

Brer Wolf Tries to Grow Horns

IT CAME ABOUT one day that all the creatures that had horns made up their minds to meet together and have a talk about how to take care of themselves—because the creatures that had teeth and claws were snatching the horned animals round every corner!

So the horned animals sent out word all round the countryside, and planned a meeting in the woods. When the day came, what a large crowd of them there was! They stamped through the bushes, they bellowed and they mooed, they grunted and they snorted. My, it was a fine crowd that met together that day.

Mr. Bull, he was there, and he took the head of the meeting. Mr. Steer was there, stamping his hoof. Miss Cow was there, whisking her tail round. Mr. Billy Goat was there, wagging his beard and talking away to Miss Cow. Mr. Unicorn was there, with his great long horn sticking right up into the air. Mr. Benjamin Ram was there, with his fiddle. And old man Rhinoceros was there too, taking up a mighty lot of room.

There were lots more, too many to tell, for they came in crowds. Old Brer Wolf, he heard about this meeting and he made up his mind he'd go along and see what it was all about—and maybe sneak off with one of Mr. Benjamin Ram's children.

But he didn't know how to go without being known as Brer Wolf. Any creature there without horns would be noticed at once and sent away with a horn in his side if he wasn't careful! So Brer Wolf sat down and thought hard. He meant to go to that meeting—but how could he go there unnoticed?

Pretty soon he grinned to himself and went out to the woods.

He cut himself two crooked sticks and tied them on his head! The sticks looked just like horns—and my, but Brer Wolf looked a mighty queer creature! He set off to the meeting, and mixed with all the crowd.

Now as he went to the meeting Brer Rabbit saw him—and he sprang aside into the bushes quickly when he saw a creature looking like Brer Wolf, yet carrying horns on his head! "My!" said Brer Rabbit to himself, "if it isn't enough that Brer Wolf's got claws and teeth—and now he's got horns as well. I wonder why."

Well, Brer Rabbit didn't mean to let Brer Wolf out of his sight, so he went after him, hiding in the bushes all the way. And pretty soon he came to the meeting too, but as he had no horns on his head Brer Rabbit kept in the bushes, and lay there without moving even an ear.

When Brer Wolf got to the meeting Mr. Bull saw him.

"Who are you?" said Mr. Bull, in surprise, for he had never seen a creature quite like Brer Wolf before.

"Baa-aa-aa!" said Brer Wolf. "I'm little Sooky Calf."

Well, Mr. Bull looked at Brer Wolf very hard over the tops of his spectacles, and Brer Wolf he put down his head and made little bleating noises as best as he could. But just then some one called Mr. Bull away, and Brer Wolf took his place among the crowd, sniffing and smelling every one.

By and by the creatures began talking and telling each other of the bad ways of toothed and clawed animals. Whilst all this was going on, a big horse-fly came sailing around, and Brer Wolf quite forgot that he was supposed to be a horned creature, and he did what no horned animal ever does—he snapped at that fly!

All this time Brer Rabbit had been hiding in the bushes watching Brer Wolf, and when he saw Brer Wolf snap at the horse-fly he laughed out loud.

Mr. Bull heard the laugh and he bellowed out angrily:

"Who's that laughing away, and showing bad manners at this meeting?"

Nobody answered at all, and there was a silence. Then Brer Rabbit shouted out:

"Oh, kittle-kattle, kittle-kattle, where are your eyes?
Whoever saw a Sooky Calf snapping at flies?"

The horned animals all looked at one another and wondered what this meant. Brer Wolf felt mighty angry with Brer Rabbit, but he couldn't do a thing about it.

Before very long something bit Brer Wolf on the back of his neck, and before he knew what he was doing he sat right down and scratched himself well with his hind foot—a thing that no cow or bull ever did!

Well, Brer Rabbit shouted with laughter once more to see him, and disturbed the meeting again. Mr. Bull bellowed away in anger—and as soon as he had stopped and there was a dead silence, Brer Rabbit sang out at the top of his voice again:

"Scritchum-scratchum, look at his paws,
See that Sooky Calf scratching with claws!"

Brer Wolf was mighty scared, but it didn't seem as if any of the horned creatures knew what Brer Rabbit meant, for they took no notice of him at all.

Brer Wolf sat down on the ground behind Mr. Benjamin Ram, hoping that Mr. Ram would hide him well from Mr. Bull's eye. He put his long tail out behind him, and Sis Cow stepped on it by mistake. Brer Wolf gave a yell, and Brer Rabbit gave a great shout of laughter again.

"Who's that a-laughing and a-spoiling the meeting?" roared Mr. Bull. Nobody spoke a word—and then old Brer Rabbit he shouted loudly again from where he was hidden in the bushes:

"Rinkum, sinkum, ride him on a rail,
That Sooky Calf's got a long, bushy tail!"

Brer Wolf crouched down behind Mr. Benjamin Ram and tried to hide his tall. Nobody seemed to take much notice of him—except Mr. Bull—and he had his eye on Brer Wolf all right! Yes—Brer Wolf noticed that Mr. Bull was looking straight at him, and he didn't like it a bit. He felt mighty scared!

The meeting went on, but Brer Wolf felt more and more scared because he saw Mr. Bull edging nearer and nearer to him through the crowd. And Brer Rabbit, he wasn't going to be quiet, not he! He shouted out at the top of his voIce:

"One and one never can make six,
Sticks aren't horns, and horns aren't sticks!"

And just about then Mr. Bull saw that Brer Wolf's horns weren't horns at all but two bits of crooked stick! He roared in a rage and ran straight at Brer Wolf. He put down his head, he did, and he ran at Brer Wolf like a thunderbolt.

Brer Wolf gave a yelp and tore away. Mr. Bull grazed his horns against Brer Wolf's sides and gave him two good cuts. My, how Brer Wolf jumped!

He rushed away from the meeting, and he was so mad with Brer Rabbit that he reckoned he would pretend that the wounds Mr. Bull had given him had killed him. So he sent word round that he was dead.

Well, Brer Rabbit thought it might well be so, for he had seen Mr. Bull's horns going straight at Brer Wolf. And he thought he would pop round to Brer Wolf's house and see if he really was dead. But he remembered how Brer Wolf had tried to trick him that way before, and he didn't go inside the house—he only put his head round the door and peeped in.

Brer Rabbit saw some of the other creatures there, and he said "howdy" to them. Then he said, "Poor Brer Wolf! So Mr. Bull killed him! Dear, dear! Tell me, folks, has Brer Wolf grinned yet?"

"No, Brer Wolf hasn't grinned," said the creatures there. "Whyever should he grin, Brer Rabbit?"

"Ah," said Brer Rabbit, "wolves are strange creatures, folks. They aren't dead till they grin. You tell me when Brer Wolf grins and I'll know he's dead for good."

Well, when Brer Wolf heard this, he wanted Brer Rabbit to think he was dead, so he grinned from ear to ear! And then, of course, Brer Rabbit knew he was alive all right, and he picked up his hat and stick and ran off for home—and every now and again he would sit down and laugh fit to kill himself!

Brer Rabbit Meets His Match

ONE TIME BRER RABBIT and Brer Turkey Buzzard thought they could go shares together. They dug up a field and planted their seed, and they weeded and they watered and their crops grew mighty well.

Brer Buzzard was pleased and he told Brer Rabbit that when they sold their crop there would be a mighty lot of money between the two of them.

Well, Brer Rabbit gathered in the crop and he set off to sell it. Brer Buzzard let him do the selling for he hadn't much head for that sort of thing. But there was a great shock for Brer Buzzard the day he asked Brer Rabbit for his share of the money.

"Brer Buzzard, I'm mighty sorry, but I've got bad news for you," said Brer Rabbit, looking sad and solemn. "That crop of ours wasn't any good at all when it came to selling."

"It looked mighty good in the field," said Brer Turkey Buzzard, puzzled.

"Yes, it did so," said Brer Rabbit. "But it fetched no money at all, Brer Buzzard, except what it cost me to sell it. I'm in a bad way, I am, Brer Buzzard, with the winter coming on, and children to feed, and no money in my pocket."

Brer Buzzard flew off, and he sat in a tree and thought hard. He made up his mind to watch Brer Rabbit carefully, and if he saw him spending money and acting gay and cheerful, Brer Buzzard reckoned he would know Brer Rabbit had deceived him over the crops.

But Brer Rabbit, he went about with a long face, and moped round till nobody liked him about. All the same, Brer Buzzard knew how tricky Brer Rabbit could be, and he didn't just believe that things were so bad as Brer Rabbit made out.

So he thought a bit more and at last he got a plan. One day he flew along to where Brer Rabbit was sitting, and shouted to him:

"Brer Rabbit! I've got a bit of luck! I've been across the river, and let me tell you there's fine rich gold-mines over there!"

"What, just across the river?" said Brer Rabbit.

"That's right," said Brer Buzzard. "You come with me, Brer Rabbit. I'll scratch in the mines and you can grabble, and between the two of us we'll get enough gold to set us up properly. I'm sorry for you, Brer Rabbit, these days—you go around looking so sad and solemn. You come and share this bit of luck with me!"

"I'd like to come," said Brer Rabbit, "but it beats me how I'll get across the river, Brer Buzzard. Every time I get my foot wet all my family catch cold!"

"That's too bad, Brer Rabbit," said Brer Buzzard. "I guess I'll have to go alone."

"How are you going to cross the river?" said Brer Rabbit.

"Oh, I shall fly," said Brer Buzzard, and he spread his big wings.

"Wait a minute, Brer Buzzard," said Brer Rabbit. "Can't you carry me across, so's I could come with you?"

"Well, I dare say I could," said Brer Buzzard, and he squatted down on the ground so that Brer Rabbit could get on his back. Then he spread his wings and rose up in the air.

But instead of flying right across the river Brer Buzzard flew to an island in the middle of it—and on this island was a tall pine-tree, and Brer Buzzard went and perched on the very topmost bough. There he sat, with Brer Rabbit clinging to his back, just about the scaredest rabbit in the whole world!

Well, as soon as Brer Rabbit found himself there he knew quite well that Brer Buzzard was tricking him, and he was mighty frightened. But he didn't show it. He spoke up kindly to Brer Buzzard.

"Whilst we're resting here, Brer Buzzard, and seeing you've been so kind to me, I've got some good news to tell you. I've got a gold-mine of my own, one that I made myself, and it wouldn't be a bad idea to go and see my mine before we bother about the one over the river."

Then old Brer Buzzard he laughed till he shook, and Brer Rabbit felt sure he would fall off and drown in the deep water running all round.

"Hold on, Brer Buzzard!" he shouted. "Don't flap your wings when you laugh, because if you do I shall drop off, and my gold-mine won't do you any good, and neither will yours do *me* any good!"

"I'm a-going to flap my wings and shake my tail and laugh till I fall off the branch myself," said old Brer Buzzard. "My, this is the best joke I've had for years, Brer Rabbit, so it is! You did me out of my fair share of money when you sold our crops, Brer Rabbit, and now I'm going to do you! Ho, ho, you thought I had a gold-mine across the river. But I haven't. I'm just a-going to laugh some more and then I'm flying off and leaving you here to study how to make crops pay next year!"

"Oh, Brer Buzzard, don't do that," said Brer Rabbit. "Pray don't do that. I'll give you some of my own money, so I will. I told you I had a gold-mine I'd made myself, didn't I? Well, I'll show you where it is."

"Yes, and that gold-mine of yours is made out of my money," said Brer Buzzard. "No, Brer Rabbit, you're a robber and a man that plays tricks on everyone. I guess folks would be pleased if I let you drop into the river right now."

"Don't you do that or you won't get any of your money or mine either," begged Brer Rabbit.

"Where have you hidden the money?" said Brer Buzzard. "Now you tell me the truth, Brer Rabbit, or I'll fly off and leave you."

"It's buried in the field by my house," said Brer Rabbit. "You fly with me there, Brer Buzzard, and I'll show you."

Well, Brer Buzzard had seen Brer Rabbit's field all dug up some days back, and he guessed Brer Rabbit was speaking the truth for once in a way. So he believed him, and told him to hold tight and he'd fly with him back to the field. Off they went, Brer Rabbit all of a shake in case Brer Buzzard should drop him by mistake.

Well, when they got to the field, Brer Rabbit turned up the earth and there was the money hidden in a box! Brer Buzzard took nearly all of it and left Brer Rabbit just a bit. As for Brer Rabbit, he had had such a scare that he didn't say a word when he saw old Brer Buzzard flying off, squawking in glee.

Poor Brer Rabbit! He walked weak in the knees for a whole month afterwards!

Brer Rabbit Gets Brer Fox's Dinner

Now, AFTER BRER RABBIT had built a steeple on his house, all the other creatures felt as if they wanted to do something to their houses too. Brer Bear put a new cellar under his, and Brer Wolf put up new window-blinds. Some chose one thing and some chose another, but old Brer Fox he took it into his head to nail new shingles on to his roof.

Brer Rabbit heard about this, and what must he do but run round and see how old Brer Fox was getting on. When he got near Brer Fox's house, he heard a mighty lamming and a blamming, and lo and behold, there was Brer Fox sitting a-straddle on the top of his roof, nailing on wooden shingles as hard as he could.

Brer Rabbit smelt something nice and he let his eye wander round Brer Fox's garden a bit. He saw Brer Fox's dinner sitting in a corner by the fence in a dinner-pail, neatly covered up. It looked so nice that Brer Rabbit's mouth began to water when he saw it, and he said to himself that he really *must* eat that dinner before he went away from there!

Then Brer Rabbit shouted up to Brer Fox, "How are you doing, Brer Fox?"

"I'm too busy to talk," said Brer Fox.

"What are you doing up there?" said Brer Rabbit.

"Putting a new roof on my house before the rain comes," said Brer Fox, hammering away.

"What time is it, Brer Fox?" asked Brer Rabbit.

"It's working-time with me, that's what it is," said Brer Fox, lamming away at his roof.

"Don't you want any help?" shouted Brer Rabbit.

"I could do with some," said Brer Fox, "though I don't know

where in the name of goodness I'm going to get any!"

With that Brer Rabbit sort of pulled at his whiskers. Then he said, "I used to be a mighty handy man with a hammer, Brer Fox, and I'm not too proud now to climb up and help you."

"I'm mighty much obliged," said Brer Fox. And no sooner had he said that than Brer Rabbit snatched off his coat, leapt up the ladder, and sat down to hammer on shingles. And he put on more shingles in an hour than Brer Fox put on in two.

Oh, he was a clever fellow, Brer Rabbit was! There wasn't any kind of work that Brer Rabbit couldn't do, and do it better than any one else too.

He nailed on shingles till he got tired, Brer Rabbit did, and all the time he was thinking how to get Brer Fox's dinner. Maybe Brer Fox would offer to share it with him—and maybe he wouldn't! Brer Rabbit nailed and nailed. He would nail one row and Brer Fox would nail one row. He caught up Brer Fox and passed him—caught him up and passed him again, till by and by, whilst he was a-nailing, Brer Fox's tail got in his way.

Brer Fox was working just above Brer Rabbit, and his tail hung down on to Brer Rabbit's row of shingles. Brer Rabbit couldn't see what he was doing, so he pushed Brer Fox's tail out of the way.

"I don't know what in the name of goodness folks have such long tails for!" he said to himself.

Soon Brer Fox's tail got in Brer Rabbit's way again. He pushed it to the side. It came back again. He pushed it away. But he hadn't more than pushed it away before it came back again.

Well, this made Brer Rabbit mighty mad. How can a man nail shingles on a roof if a big tail is in the way all the time? "If this tail doesn't get out of my way I'll have to do something about it," said Brer Rabbit to himself. And at that, down came the tail again and nearly knocked Brer Rabbit's hammer out of his hand.

Well, there was only one thing to do—and Brer Rabbit did it. He nailed Brer Fox's tail to the roof, and then he went on working, glad that the tail wasn't in his way any more. Well, they nailed and they nailed—and bless gracious, it wasn't long before Brer Fox tried to move along, and found that he couldn't! He dropped everything and squalled out:

"Lawks-amussy, Brer Rabbit! You've nailed my tail down! You've nailed my tail down!"

Brer Rabbit stopped hammering. He winked first one eye and then the other, and rubbed his forehead as if he were mighty puzzled.

"Surely I haven't nailed your tail, Brer Fox! Surely I haven't! Look close and see, Brer Fox, but be careful you don't fall. For goodness' sake don't say I've nailed your tail, Brer Fox, if I haven't!"

Brer Fox shouted and yelled, and squealed and kicked.

"Lawks-amussy, Brer Rabbit! I tell you, you have nailed my tail down! Un-nail me, Brer Rabbit, un-nail me!"

Brer Rabbit made for the ladder and started down it. He looked up at Brer Fox as if he was mighty sorry, and he said:

"Well, well, well! Just to think I should have been so careless as to nail Brer Fox's tail down! I don't know when I've heard

51

anything that made me feel so mighty bad. If I hadn't seen it with my own eyes I wouldn't have believed it, that I wouldn't."

Well, Brer Fox yelled, Brer Fox howled, but it wasn't a bit of good. There he was up on the roof with his tail nailed down hard and fast. Brer Rabbit, he kept on talking all the time he was going down the ladder.

"It makes me feel so bad," he said, "that I don't know what to do. Every time I think of it I feel an empty place come in my middle."

By this time Brer Rabbit was down on the ground, and whilst Brer Fox was yelling, he just kept on talking.

"Yes, there's a mighty empty place in my middle," he said, "and if I don't make a mistake, why, here's a tin-pail full of dinner in the corner over there that will just about fit that empty place!"

With that Brer Rabbit ran to the pail, took off the lid, sat down and began to eat. He ate up the greens, he ate up the meat, and he drank the gravy. Then he wiped his mouth on his coat-tail and said:

"I don't know when I've been so sorry about anything as I am about Brer Fox's nice long tail. Surely, surely, I must have been dreaming when I nailed Brer Fox's fine long tail," said old Brer Rabbit.

And then he skipped out of the garden, Brer Rabbit did, and it wasn't long before he was safely at home, telling his old woman how sorry he was about Brer Fox's lovely long tail.

As for old Brer Fox, he had to sit up on his roof till Brer Wolf came by and un-nailed him. Poor Brer Fox! He might have known Brer Rabbit would trick him somehow.

Brer Rabbit Saves Brer Terrapin

ONE TIME BRER FOX was going down the big road and he saw old Brer Terrapin going to his home. Now Brer Fox knew Brer Terrapin was a good friend to Brer Rabbit, and it seemed to him it was a mighty good time to catch him. Brer Fox didn't have any kindly feelings towards people who were friends of Brer Rabbit.

Brer Fox ran back to his own house, which was not far off, and got a bag. Then he ran down the road again, rushed up behind Brer Terrapin, caught him up and threw him into the bag. He slung the bag across his back, then off he went, galloping home.

Brer Terrapin, he shouted, but it wasn't any good. He wriggled and struggled, but that wasn't any good either. Brer Fox just went on going, and there was old Brer Terrapin in the corner of the bag, and the bag tied up hard and fast

But where was Brer Rabbit whilst all this was going on? Where was that long-eared, hoppetty-skippetty creature, that up-and-down-and-sailing-round Brer Rabbit? He wasn't far off, you may be sure!

Brer Fox went trotting down the big road with the bag on his back—and Brer Rabbit was sitting in the bushes just by the side of the road. He saw Brer Fox trotting by and he saw the bag on his back too.

"Now what's Brer Fox got in that bag?" said Brer Rabbit to himself. "I don't know what it can be."

Well, Brer Rabbit sat in the bushes and wondered and wondered, but the more he wondered the less he could think what it was. He watched Brer Fox a-trotting down the road, and still he sat in the bushes and wondered.

"Huh!" said Brer Rabbit at last, "Brer Fox has no business to be trotting down the road carrying something other people don't know about. I guess I'll go after Brer Fox and find out what's in the bag!"

With that, Brer Rabbit set out. He hadn't got a bag to carry and he went mighty quickly. He took a short cut, and by the time Brer Fox got to his house Brer Rabbit had had time to get into his strawberry-bed and trample down a whole lot of plants. When he had done that, he sat down in some bushes where he could see Brer Fox coming home.

By and by Brer Fox came along with his bag across his back. He unlatched his door, he did, and then he threw Brer Terrapin down in a corner in the bag, and sat down to rest himself, for Brer Terrapin was mighty heavy to carry.

Brer Fox had hardly put a match to his pipe when Brer Rabbit stuck his head in at the door and shouted:

"Brer Fox! Oh, Brer Fox! You'd better take your stick and run out yonder. Coming along just now I heard a fuss going on in your garden, and I looked round and there were a whole lot of folk in your strawberry-bed, just a-trampling the strawberries down! I shouted at them, but they didn't take any notice of a little man like me. Make haste, Brer Fox make haste! Get your stick and run. I'd go with you too, but I've got to get home. You'd better hurry, Brer Fox, if you want to save your strawberries. Run, Brer Fox, run!"

With that Brer Rabbit darted back into the bushes, and Brer Fox dropped his pipe and grabbed his stick and rushed out to his strawberry-bed. And no sooner was he gone than old Brer Rabbit hopped out of the bushes and into the house.

He didn't make a bit of noise. He looked round and there was the bag in the corner. He caught hold of it and felt it to see what was inside. And suddenly something yelled:

"Ow! Go away! Let me alone! Turn me loose! Ow!"

Brer Rabbit jumped back astonished. Then before you could

wink an eye he slapped himself on the leg and laughed out loud.

"If I'm not making a mistake, that's nobody's voice but old Brer Terrapin's!" said Brer Rabbit.

"Is that Brer Rabbit?" yelled Brer Terrapin.

"It is," said Brer Rabbit.

"Then hurry up and get me out," said Brer Terrapin. "There's dust in my throat, grit in my eyes, and I can hardly breathe. Get me out, Brer Rabbit."

"Heyo, Brer Terrapin," said Brer Rabbit. "You're a lot smarter than I am—because here you are in a bag and I don't know how in the name of goodness you've tied yourself up in there, that I don't!"

Brer Terrapin tried to explain and Brer Rabbit kept on laughing, but all the same he untied the bag, took Brer Terrapin out and carried him outside the gate. Then, when he had done this, Brer Rabbit ran off to where he knew some wasps had a nest just about as big as a football.

The wasp-nest was in a hollow tree. Brer Rabbit slipped in at the bottom of the tree and there was the nest inside. He slapped his paw over the hole where the wasps went in and out, knocked the nest down into his bag, and there he had it, wasps and all!

Then back he raced to Brer Fox's house and flung the bag down on the floor, tied up fast. Well, the way he slammed that bag down on the floor stirred all those wasps up and put them into a very bad temper! They buzzed fit to make holes in the bag!

Soon Brer Rabbit saw Brer Fox coming down the back-garden, where he had been looking for the folks that had trodden down his strawberries. He had been putting the plants straight and picking off the squashed fruit, and Brer Fox was feeling mighty mad about it too.

By the time Brer Fox got indoors Brer Rabbit was off and away into a bush—and there he sat with old Brer Terrapin, waiting to see what would happen.

Brer Fox went indoors, hitting the ground with his stick, and vowing that he would shake Brer Terrapin to bits, he was in such a bad temper.

He slammed the door and Brer Rabbit and Brer Terrapin waited. They listened, but at first they couldn't hear anything. By and by they heard the most tremendous noise!

"Seems like a whole crowd of cows running round and round inside Brer Fox's house," Brer Rabbit said to Brer Terrapin.

"I can hear chairs a-falling," said Brer Terrapin.

"I can hear the table turning over," said Brer Rabbit.

"I can hear the crockery smashing," said Brer Terrapin.

"Huh!" said Brer Rabbit, enjoying himself, "Brer Fox must be having a fine game with those wasps. What a surprise he got when he opened the bag to get you—and found a wasp's nest instead!"

Just as Brer Rabbit said that, Brer Fox's door flew wide open and out rushed Brer Fox, squalling and howling as if two hundred dogs had got him by the tail!

He ran straight to the river, he did, and plunged in to get rid of the wasps on him. Brer Rabbit and Brer Terrapin sat there in the bushes and laughed and laughed, till by and by Brer Rabbit rolled over and said:

"One more laugh, Brer Terrapin, and you'll have to carry me home!"

"Get on my back then, Brer Rabbit, get on my back," said Brer Terrapin. "I'll carry you all right. Shoo! That will teach Brer Fox not to go a-catching an old fellow like me and putting him into a dusty bag!"

Brer Fox came out of the river at last—but to this day he doesn't know how it was that though he put old Brer Terrapin into a bag, it was a nest of wasps that came out! And you may be sure Brer Rabbit never told him!

Mr. Benjamin Ram

OLD MR. BENJAMIN RAM was a queer-looking creature, he surely was. His wrinkly horn and the shaggy hair on his neck made him look mighty fierce, and when he shook his head and snorted it looked as if he were going to paw up all the ground beneath his feet!

Old Brer Fox had been catching and eating Mr. Benjamin Ram's children, the little lambs, but he had never got too close to Mr. Ram himself.

One time when he was going down the road, talking to Brer Wolf, Brer Fox let out a big sigh and said he was mighty hungry in his middle.

"Why in the name of goodness are you hungry, Brer Fox, when old Mr. Benjamin Ram is up in his house there just rolling in fat?" said Brer Wolf, in an astonished voice.

"Huh!" said Brer Fox, "I know I'm in the habit of eating Mr. Ram's children, but I'm sort of scared of the old creature because of his red eye and wrinkly horn."

Brer Wolf shouted with laughter, and said, "Good gracious, Brer Fox! I don't know what sort of a fellow you are—why, that old Mr. Ram never hurt a fly in all his life, that he hasn't!"

Brer Fox looked very hard at Brer Wolf. Then he said, "Heyo, Brer Wolf! Many's the time I've seen you hungry, but yet I never heard you talk of making a meal off Mr. Benjamin Ram!"

Brer Wolf didn't quite know what to say to this. After a bit he said, "I should just like to know who in the name of goodness would want to eat a tough old creature like Mr. Benjamin Ram! I'd just like to know that, Brer Fox!"

Brer Fox laughed, he did, and then he said to Brer Wolf, "Ah, yi, Brer Wolf! You ask me what I go hungry for when

I could go and eat old Mr. Benjamin Ram—but why didn't *you* eat him when *you* were hungry? That's what I want to know!"

Brer Wolf got angry and hit the ground with the end of his stick. "I've said all I've got to say," he said. "That old creature is too tough for me to eat."

Although he was very hungry, Brer Fox went on laughing. "Well, Brer Wolf," he said, "I'm not going to talk about it any longer—I'm going to do what you say. I'm going to go up to Mr. Ram's house and have him for supper—and I wish you'd be so good as to go along and keep me company."

Well, Brer Wolf didn't like the sound of this at all. "I'd rather go by myself," he said.

"Well, you'd better hurry then," said Brer Fox, "because it isn't going to take me long to get to Mr. Ram's house!"

Brer Wolf was in a fix. He knew quite well that if he backed out of this, Brer Fox would tell Miss Meadows and the girls, and they would laugh at him and tease him. So he marched off towards Mr. Benjamin Ram's house.

As he went, a little puff of wind blew up some leaves, and they scared Brer Wolf so much that he jumped as if he had been shot. Brer Fox laughed at him, and this made Brer Wolf so angry that he hurried on in front to Mr. Ram's house.

He knocked at the door, he did, and, of course, he expected somebody to come and open it—but instead of that, round the corner of the house came old Mr. Benjamin Ram. There he was—red eye, wrinkly horn, and shaggy head. My, what a shock he gave Brer Wolf! Brer Wolf shot down the path, and out of the gate back to Brer Fox as if he'd been fired out of a gun!

Brer Fox laughed and laughed. Brer Wolf looked mighty down in the dumps. "Have you killed and eaten Mr. Benjamin Ram?" asked Brer Fox. "And have you left any for me?"

"Be quiet," said Brer Wolf. "I'm not feeling very well."

"Well, your legs feel well enough!" said Brer Fox. " My, how they ran just now!"

"I only ran to see if I could make myself feel better," said Brer Wolf sulkily.

"Dear, dear!" said Brer Fox. "When *I'm* feeling poorly, Brer Wolf, I just want to lie down!"

Well, they went on this way, they did, till by and by Brer Fox asked Brer Wolf if he would go with him to catch Mr. Benjamin Ram.

"No, Brer Fox," said Brer Wolf. "I'm afraid you'll run off and leave me to do the fighting."

"Indeed I won't," said Brer Fox. "And I'll soon show you how to feel safe. I'll get a rope and tie one end to you and one end to me. Then we can neither of us run away! We'll both have to fight!"

Well, Brer Wolf had to be content with that, and they set out to Mr. Benjamin Ram's house. Brer Wolf sort of hung back, but he was ashamed to say he was afraid, and on they went until they got right up to Mr. Ram's house.

When they got there the old creature was sitting out in the front porch sunning himself. He saw them coming and cleared his throat and shouted:

"Ha, Brer Fox! I see you've got Brer Wolf tied up properly, and you're a-leading him here to me! I'm obliged to you for catching him for me. My larder is getting empty, and I'd like to chop him up and pickle him. Fetch him in, Brer Fox, fetch him in!"

Just about then Mrs. Ram looked out of the window and saw the two coming, and she was so scared that she began to bleat at the top of her voice! My! You should have heard her! Her voice even reached the town, it was so loud. It even scared Mr. Benjamin Ram himself, but he kept on talking.

"Fetch him in, Brer Fox! Fetch him in! Don't you hear my old woman bleating for him? She hasn't tasted wolf-meat for years. My, won't she be pleased to have some on her table. Fetch him in, Brer Fox, fetch him in!"

Well, when Brer Wolf heard all this he got more scared than ever. First he tried to untie the rope round him, and when he couldn't do it, he turned back and ran for his life, jerking poor Brer Fox off his feet, and dragging him behind him at the other end of the rope as if he were a parcel of bones!

Bumpity-thumpity-bump! Thumpity-bumpity-thump! Brer Fox bumped and thumped over the ground till the rope broke—and then he sat up and saw Brer Wolf disappearing in the wood like a streak of lightning.

And that was the last time Brer Fox tried any tricks with Mr. Benjamin Ram. My, what a crowd of fine bruises and bumps he had that day!

Brer Rabbit Saves His Meat

ONE TIME BRER WOLF was coming along home after he had been fishing. He sauntered along the road, with his string of fish across his shoulder, when suddenly he saw old Miss Partridge scrambling round in the bushes. She was trying to take him away from her nest, which was not far off. She hopped out of the bushes and fluttered right along just under Brer Wolf's nose.

Well, Brer Wolf guessed old Miss Partridge was trying to get him away from her nest, so he put down his string of fish and began to hunt about in the bushes for the young birds.

About that time Brer Rabbit happened along. There were the fishes—and there was Brer Rabbit. But when Brer Wolf came out of the bushes, there were no fishes to be seen—and no Brer Rabbit either!

Brer Wolf sat down and scratched his head, and wondered what could have happened to his fishes. Then he suddenly thought that Brer Rabbit must have been along there. So Brer Wolf set out for Brer Rabbit's house and when he got there he shouted for him.

"Brer Rabbit! Have you taken my fishes?"

"What fishes?" said Brer Rabbit.

"My string of fishes I left away back in the wood," said Brer Wolf. "Now, Brer Rabbit, just you tell me the truth. I know you took my fishes."

Well, they argued up and down. Brer Wolf said Brer Rabbit had his fishes, and Brer Rabbit said he hadn't. And then Brer Rabbit got mad and said:

"Well, if you think I've got those fishes of yours, Brer Wolf, I give you leave to kill my best cow!"

Brer Rabbit didn't for one minute think Brer Wolf would

take him at his word—but Brer Wolf did! He went straight-away to the fields, drove up Brer Rabbit's cattle, and killed Brer Rabbit's best cow.

Brer Rabbit felt mighty bad at losing his cow, but he laid his plans, and he told his children that Brer Wolf might kill his

cow, but he wasn't going to eat the meat! No, he would see that his own family ate cow-meat before many days were out.

So Brer Rabbit rushed up to the field shouting loudly: "Brer Wolf! Brer Wolf! Here come the dogs! Run and hide, quickly! The dogs will get you! I'll look after the cow for you till you come back!"

Brer Wolf got such a fright that he shot off into the bushes like a bullet out of a gun. He was hardly out of sight before Brer Rabbit ran up to the cow, took it away, and put it into the smoke-house for meat. When he had done this he took the cow's tail and stuck the end of it hard into the ground.

Then he yelled out for Brer Wolf.

"Brer Wolf! Brer Wolf! Run here! Your cow's going into the ground! Run quickly!"

When old Brer Wolf got there, which he did in half a minute, he saw Brer Rabbit holding on to the end of the cow-tail, as if he was trying to keep it from going into the ground. Brer Wolf really thought that the cow had run right into the ground and that only her tail was sticking out, and he caught hold of it in a trice. He pulled and pulled to get the cow out—but all that happened was that the tail suddenly shot up from the earth and Brer Wolf sat down very hard.

Then Brer Rabbit winked at his children and said, "There! The tail's pulled out and the cow's gone!"

But Brer Wolf wasn't one to give up easily. He fetched a spade and a pick-axe and a shovel and he dug and dug for that cow till he couldn't dig any more.

Old Brer Rabbit he sat up in his front porch, smoking his cigar. And every time Brer Wolf stuck his pick-axe in the clay Brer Rabbit giggled to his children and said:

"He diggy, diggy, diggy, but there's no meat there! He diggy, diggy, diggy, but there's no meat there!"

And all the time the cow was lying in the smoke-house and Brer Rabbit and his children were eating fried beef and onions every time they were hungry. Poor Brer Wolf! He had lost both his fishes and his cow!

Brer Bear Gets a Shock

ONE TIME BRER BEAR went to look at his honey store and he found that half his honey-jars were empty. Well, he ranted and he roared, he howled and he stamped, and he vowed he'd find the thief if it took him a month of Sundays.

He went stamping out of his house, and who should he meet but old Brer Wolf, come to see if Brer Bear was away from home—for Brer Wolf liked a lick of honey himself, and he was the thief all right!

"Someone's been at my honey, Brer Wolf—someone's been at my honey!" roared Brer Bear. "Who do you think it can be? I'm just going to squeeze the life out of him!"

Brer Wolf looked alarmed. He didn't want to be squeezed in Brer Bear's big arms! "Well," he said, "I saw that rascal of a Brer Rabbit the other day with honey on his whiskers. Ah, yes, Brer Bear, sure enough you'll find it's Brer Rabbit who's the thief!"

"I thought as much!" yelled Brer Bear in a rage. "He's always where he shouldn't be. But he's played his tricks once too often!"

He rushed off to find Brer Rabbit, and as he went through the wood, what did he see but old Brer Rabbit sitting on a tree-stump combing his fine whiskers.

"Are you combing the honey out of your whiskers?" shouted Brer Bear, and he rushed at Brer Rabbit.

"Now, now, Brer Bear!" cried Brer Rabbit, in alarm, as Brer Bear knocked him over. "What's the matter? Can't I comb my whiskers?"

"Not if they've got my honey on them!" roared Brer Bear angrily. "I'm going to squeeze you, Brer Rabbit—yes, I'm going to squeeze you, and make you say where you've put all my honey!"

Brer Wolf crept up and saw the fight. He rubbed his paws in glee, for he guessed that old Brer Rabbit wouldn't come bobbing up *this* time! Brer Bear got hold of Brer Rabbit and began to hug him so that he couldn't breathe.

"Stop it, Brer Bear, stop it!" panted poor Brer Rabbit. "I tell you, I don't know anything about your honey."

"Now you just tell me where you've put my honey and I'll let you go," said Brer Bear. "Go on—tell me. If you don't, I'll squeeze you to bits!"

Well, Brer Rabbit could see that Brer Bear meant what he said all right, and he began to think how he could stop him.

"Brer Bear, Brer Bear, how can I tell you where your honey is if you squeeze all my breath out of me!" panted Brer Rabbit.

Brer Bear stopped squeezing quite so hard. "Will you tell me, Brer Rabbit?" he said.

"Brer Bear, I'm not certain where your honey is, but I think maybe you'll get a nice surprise if you look into that hollow tree that's growing by the pond in the wood," said Brer Rabbit, trying to get his breath again.

"Are you sure I shall get a surprise if I look there?" asked Brer Bear squeezing Brer Rabbit tightly again.

"Brer Bear, stop hugging me!" begged Brer Rabbit in alarm. "You're squeezing my chest right through my back! I tell you, you'll surely get a fine surprise if you look inside that tree!"

Brer Bear let Brer Rabbit go. He ambled off to the tree, and Brer Wolf and Brer Rabbit followed him, though poor Brer Rabbit could hardly walk.

Well, Brer Bear, he got to the hollow tree all right. He climbed up to where the hole was, and put in his paw. But it was a very deep hole and he could feel nothing.

"Get down into the hole, Brer Bear, get down into the hole!" squealed Brer Rabbit. So Brer Bear jumped right down into the hole, and pawed about for the honey.

But in that hole lived Cousin Wildcat, his wife, and his

family—and when old Brer Bear jumped right down up top of the lot of them, there was a great disturbance!

My goodness! All those wildcats shot out their twenty claws, and clawed at Brer Bear. Cousin Wildcat and his wife buried their sharp teeth into his paws, and before Brer Bear knew what was happening he was in the middle of a fierce fight!

"Ooooph! Grumph! Ow-wow-wow!" growled Brer Bear.

"Yee-ow-yee-ow, yee-ow!" yelled all the wildcats together.

Brer Bear shot out of that hollow tree a whole lot quicker than he went in! My, how quickly he came out! Brer Rabbit had never seen a bear move so quickly!

"You said I'd find my honey there!" roared Brer Bear to Brer Rabbit.

"I didn't!" yelled back cheeky Brer Rabbit. "I just said you'd get a fine surprise if you looked in that hollow tree. But if you want to find the thief, Brer Bear, just come and look at Brer Wolf here! He's got honey on his nose—and I guess he's been after yours!"

And with that Brer Rabbit turned and ran, and old Brer Wolf, he got such a slap on the nose from angry Brer Bear that he yowled like a hundred wildcats at once!

As for Brer Bear, he wouldn't go near a hollow tree for months, not even when he saw bees coming out of it and knew there was honey there. No—he was much too afraid of getting another fine surprise!

Brer Rabbit Raises the Dust

Now ONE TIME it happened that Brer Fox and Brer Rabbit, Brer Wolf, Brer Bear and the rest were always up at Miss Meadows'. When Miss Meadows had chicken for dinner in would come Brer Fox and Brer Possum, and when she had fried greens in would come Brer Rabbit. If she had new honey it would be Brer Bear that would come popping his head round the door.

"I can't feed everyone," said Miss Meadows to the girls. "It's getting to be a real nuisance, having all the creatures pestering round. We shall have to do something to stop them."

Well, Miss Meadows and the girls, they thought what they could do to stop the animals coming so much. And they decided that the one that could knock the most dust out of a rock, he should be the one that could still come to Miss Meadows' house. The rest must stay away.

So Miss Meadows told everyone that if they would come to her house the next Saturday evening, the whole crowd of them would go down the road to where there was a big flint rock. And each of them could take up the sledge-hammer and see how much dust he could raise out of the rock.

"I shall knock out a cloud of dust!" said Brer Fox.

"You won't be able to see for miles round when I get going with that sledge-hammer!" boasted old Brer Bear.

Well, they all talked mighty biggitty except Brer Rabbit. He crept off to a cool place and there he sat down and puzzled out how he could raise dust out of a rock. He had never seen dust got out of a rock, and he guessed he never would. But he meant to do it somehow.

By and by, whilst he was a-sitting there, up he jumped and cracked his heels together and sang out:

"Brer Buzzard is clever, and so is Brer Fox,
But Brer Rabbit makes them all pull up their socks!"

And with that he set out for Brer Raccoon's house and borrowed his slippers. When Saturday night came everyone was up at Miss Meadows' house. Miss Meadows and the girls were there; and Brer Raccoon, Brer Fox, Brer Wolf, Brer Bear, Brer Possum and Brer Terrapin. They were all there.

Brer Rabbit shuffled up late. By the time he got to the house, everyone had gone down the road to the rock. Brer Rabbit was waiting for that—and as soon as he knew no one was at home, he crept round to the ash-bin, and filled Brer Raccoon's slippers full of ashes, and then he put them on his feet and marched off!

Brer Rabbit got to the rock after a while, and as soon as Miss Meadows and the girls saw him they began to giggle and laugh because of the great big old slippers he had on.

Brer Fox laughed too, and thought of something smart to say. "I guess old Brer Rabbit's got chilblains," he said. "He's getting old."

But Brer Rabbit winked his eye at everybody and said: "You know, folks, I've been so used to riding on horseback, as these ladies know, that I'm getting sort of tender-footed when I walk."

Then Brer Fox, he remembered how Brer Rabbit had ridden him one day, and he didn't say another word more. Everybody began to giggle, and it looked as if they would never begin hammering on the rock. Brer Rabbit picked up the sledge-hammer as if he meant to have the first try. But Brer Fox shoved Brer Rabbit out of the way and took the sledge-hammer himself.

Everyone was to have three hits at the rock with the hammer, and the one that raised the most dust out of it was the one who would be allowed to go to Miss Meadows' house as often as he liked. All the others were to keep away.

Well, old Brer Fox, he grabbed the hammer, he did, and he

brought it down on the rock—*blim*! No dust came. Then he drew back the hammer and down he came again on the rock—*blam*! Still no dust came. Then he spat on his hands, gave a big swing and down came the hammer—*ker-blap*! And still not a speck of dust flew!

That was Brer Fox's turn finished. Then Brer Possum had a try, but he didn't raise any dust either. After that Brer Raccoon took the hammer, and he tried, but he couldn't make a speck of dust come at all. Then everyone else had a try except Brer Terrapin and Brer Rabbit, but nobody raised any dust at all.

"Now it's your turn, Brer Terrapin," said Brer Fox.

But Brer Terrapin, he said no. He had watched the mighty blows the others had given for nothing, and he wasn't going to tire himself out too.

"I've got a crick in my neck," he said. "I don't think I'll take my turn. Let Brer Rabbit have his. Looks like we'll none of us be able to raise any dust—so Miss Meadows and the girls won't have the pleasure of anybody's visit!"

Brer Rabbit winked to himself, and grabbed hold of the sledge-hammer. He lifted it up into the air, and as he brought it down on the rock he jumped up and came down at the same time as the hammer—*pow*! And, of course, the ashes flew up out of his slippers and shot all round.

Brer Fox, he started sneezing away because the ashes got up his nose, and Miss Meadows and the girls they began to cough and splutter.

Then Brer Rabbit lifted up the hammer again, jumped high into the air and landed on the rock with his feet and the hammer at the same time—*kerblam*!

"Stand further off, ladies!" he yelled. "Here comes the dust!"

And sure enough the dust came, for the ashes flew again out of his slippers and everyone sneezed and choked and rubbed their eyes!

Then once more Brer Rabbit jumped up and cracked his

heels together and brought the hammer down on the rock—
kerblam! "Here comes the dust!" he yelled. And sure enough,
the dust came!

Well, after that there wasn't much doubt about who should
be the one to visit Miss Meadows and the girls, and Brer Rabbit
went off arm-in-arm with two of the girls, grinning at all the
others. They stood there, blowing their noses and glaring at Brer
Rabbit; and Brer Fox, he took a sneezing fit and couldn't stop
till the next morning.

Brer Raccoon got his slippers back from Brer Rabbit all
right, and nobody ever knew what Brer Rabbit had borrowed
them for. Cunning old Brer Rabbit! There wasn't much he
didn't know!

Brer Wolf Gets Too Warm

NOW AFTER BRER FOX got hit on the nose by Cousin Wildcat it was a mighty long time before he could ramble round and worry old Brer Rabbit. For one thing, Brer Fox had to wear a bandage on his nose, and this didn't make him very beautiful, so he kept at home. But after a while he went out and told every one how Brer Rabbit had tricked him into fighting the fierce wildcat.

Well, Brer Fox told his story so well that all the other creatures agreed that Brer Rabbit was getting worse and worse. Brer Wolf got up and said the time was come when no one should be friends with Brer Rabbit.

"We won't drink out of the same stream as he does, nor walk in the same road, nor live near him, nor go washing in the same washing-hole!" said Brer Wolf.

"We certainly won't!" shouted all the creatures. "And if we can get hold of that wicked Brer Rabbit, we will. It's time his tricks came to an end."

Well, Brer Rabbit couldn't help noticing all these things, for when he met some one in the big road they turned off into the wood before he came up to them—and if he shouted "How-do!" to any one, they didn't answer. It seemed as if Brer Rabbit hadn't any friends at all.

Brer Rabbit guessed he had better make his house a bit stronger. So he worked on his windows and made them fine and strong and put a new bolt on his door. And then, bless us all, if he didn't take it into his head to build a steeple on the top of his house! Yes, a sure-enough steeple, so high that folks going along the big road stopped and said—"Hey! What kind of town-hall is that?"

Well, folks stopped and asked, but Brer Rabbit hadn't got

time to answer. He hammered and he nailed, he knocked and he lammed! Folks went by but he didn't say a word to them. Creatures stood round to watch him, but he didn't look at them. It was work, work, work, from sun-up to sun-down, till that steeple got done.

Then old Brer Rabbit drew a long breath, wiped his forehead, and said: "Well, if any one can come and catch me now, I'd like to see it!"

With that he went and got something to eat, and he got a long piece of plough-line too, and he told his old woman to put a kettle of water on the fire, and to stand close by.

"And mind this, old woman," he said, "whatever I tell you not to do, you do it. Have you got that? What I tell you not to do, is just what you *must* do!"

Then old Brer Rabbit took his rocking-chair up into the big steeple, near the window there, and sat down and looked out.

It wasn't long before every one heard that Brer Rabbit had stopped work, and they came around to see what he meant to do next. But Brer Rabbit, he just sat up there, smoking his cigar, looking out and thinking. Brer Wolf stood up and looked at the steeple, Brer Fox he stood up to look at it too, and so did Brer Bear. All the other creatures did the same. They walked round and nudged one another, and stared and stared. All the time old Brer Rabbit sat up there, smoking his cigar, and looking out and thinking.

By and by old Brer Terrapin came along. Now old Brer Terrapin had been friendly with Brer Rabbit so long that he guessed at once there was soon going to be some fun. He laughed right down under the roof of his house, Brer Terrapin did, and then he called to Brer Rabbit:

"Heyo, Brer Rabbit! What are you doing away up there?"

"I'm just a-resting myself, Brer Terrapin," said Brer Rabbit. "Do come up and see me."

"Well, between you and me, Brer Rabbit," said Brer

Terrapin, "I'd find it mighty difficult to climb so high. Suppose you come down here and see me! If you live so high up you might as well grow wings! I'm afraid I can't stretch up and shake hands with you today, Brer Rabbit!"

"Don't worry, Brer Terrapin!" said Brer Rabbit. "I've a mighty good staircase, and I'll just let it down for you."

With that Brer Rabbit let down his plough-line. "Just catch hold of that, Brer Terrapin," he said, "and up you'll come, *linkum, sinkum, binkum, boo*!"

Old Brer Terrapin knew quite well that Brer Rabbit was friendly towards him, so he wasn't afraid. But all the same, before he let himself go up on that plough-line he took it into his mouth and pulled on it to make sure it wouldn't break. Then Brer Rabbit shouted out: "Swing on, Brer Terrapin!" And Brer Terrapin, he took hold and swung on. Brer Rabbit heaved him up, and soon he was sitting up there in the steeple by the side of Brer Rabbit. But my! How funny he looked when Brer Rabbit was hauling him up, with his tail a-wiggling, and his legs all spraddled out, whirling round and round on the rope and looking mighty scared!

The other creatures saw Brer Terrapin go up safe and sound, and they saw food being passed round and lemonade, and they began to feel that they would like to see the inside of Brer Rabbit's steeple too. Brer Wolf shouted up:

"Heyo there, Brer Rabbit! You're looking mighty comfy up there! How are you?"

Brer Rabbit looked down to see who it was shouting, and when he saw it was Brer Wolf, he winked one eye to himself.

"I'm just so-so, Brer Wolf, but I can eat my food all right. Won't you come up and see me, Brer Wolf?"

"It's a mighty clumsy journey for me to make, Brer Rabbit," said Brer Wolf, "but I'll have a try!"

With that Brer Rabbit let down his plough-line, and Brer Wolf caught hold, grinning to himself at the thought of being alone with Brer Rabbit in his steeple. He could make short work of him there!

Brer Rabbit hauled on the rope and Brer Wolf went up. Brer Rabbit hauled and hauled, and when Brer Wolf was almost at the top he heard Brer Rabbit yell out to his old woman:

"Stir round, old woman, and set the table, for here's old Brer Wolf coming to dinner! But before you set the table fetch the kettle to make the coffee."

Brer Rabbit hauled and he hauled on the plough-line, and then Brer Wolf heard Brer Rabbit squall out: "Look out there, with that kettle, old woman! Don't you spill any boiling water on Brer Wolf!"

Well, that was about all that Brer Wolf heard, because the next minute down came some boiling water on him, and Brer Wolf gave a loud squeal and let go the rope! He fell down and bounced on the ground like a rubber ball.

Old Brer Rabbit leaned out of his steeple and said he was sorry his old woman had been so careless. "You heard me tell her not to scald you, Brer Wolf!" he shouted.

But no matter how much Brer Rabbit said he was sorry, it didn't make the hair come back on Brer Wolf's coat, where the water hit it.

And when the creatures had all gone, Brer Rabbit and Brer Terrapin had a mighty good laughing-spell. Brer Terrapin might have fallen out of the steeple with laughing, but Brer Rabbit caught hold of his tail just in time!

Brer Bear's Tail

THERE CAME A TIME when Brer Rabbit and Brer Terrapin became very friendly, and went about together trying to trick all the other creatures. There wasn't a day passed but Brer Rabbit called on Brer Terrapin to ask him "Howdy", or Brer Terrapin called on Brer Rabbit.

One time Brer Rabbit paid a call on Brer Terrapin, but when he got to the house Miss Terrapin told him that Brer Terrapin had gone to visit his uncle, Mr. Mud Turtle. So Brer Rabbit set out after Brer Terrapin, and when he got to Mr. Mud Turtle's house, he sat with them there and told tales till it was twelve o'clock, and dinner-time. They had crawfish for dinner, and enjoyed themselves very much.

"Now let's all go down to my mill-pond," said Mr. Mud Turtle. "There's a great big slanting rock there, and it would be fun to slide down it from the top to the bottom—and go into the water—*splash!*"

"That's so," said Brer Terrapin. "It's a mighty slippery rock, that. We'll have some fun!"

So they went off to the mill-pond and Mr. Mud Turtle took the first turn. He crawled right up to the very top of the big slanting rock, tucked his head and his legs into his shell, let himself go and down he went over the green, slippery rock into the water—*kersplash!*

Then old Brer Terrapin took a turn. He climbed right up to the very top, tucked in his head and his legs, and slid off. Down he sailed into the water—*kersplash!*

Brer Rabbit sat on a rock near by and watched them. He praised them up and begged them to do it again.

"You go on sliding, Mr. Mud Turtle," he said. "It's a fine

thing to see you coming down that rock—*swish*—*kersplash!* You do it again, Mr. Mud Turtle."

Well, Brer Terrapin and Mr. Mud Turtle they went on slipping and sliding and splashing, and Brer Rabbit, he sat by and laughed and clapped for all he was worth. And whilst they were having fun, along came old Brer Bear. He had heard them shouting and laughing and he came to see what they were doing.

"Heyo, folks !" he called. " What's all this? If my eye doesn't deceive me, here's Brer Rabbit, and Brer Terrapin, and Uncle Tommy Mud Turtle!"

"That's right," said Brer Rabbit. "And we're properly enjoying ourselves, Brer Bear!"

"Well, well, well," said Brer Bear. "So you're a-slipping and sliding, are you? And what's the matter with you, Brer Rabbit, that you're not joining in?"

Old Brer Rabbit winked hard at Brer Terrapin, and Brer Terrapin gave Mr. Mud Turtle a nudge. Here was a chance for playing a trick on old Brer Bear, sure enough!

"My goodness, Brer Bear!" said Brer Rabbit. "You can't expect a man to slip and slide the whole day, can you? I've had my fun, and now I'm a-sitting here on this rock to let my clothes dry. We're taking turn and turn about, and now it's my turn to sit out."

"Perhaps Brer Bear would like to join in with us," said Brer Terrapin.

Brer Rabbit began to shout and laugh at this. "Shoo!" he said. "Brer Bear's feet are too big and his tail is too long for him to slide down that rock!"

Well, Brer Bear didn't like this. So he spoke up at once.

"My feet may be big and my tail may be long, but I'm not afraid to try slipping and sliding down that rock!"

With that the others made room for him, and old Brer Bear, he climbed up on to the top of the rock, he did, and squatted down. He curled his tail under him and pushed off.

First he went slowly, and he grinned as if he felt mighty good; then he went a bit more quickly, and he grinned as if he felt bad; then he went very quickly, and he grinned as if he felt mighty scared; and then he came to the green and very slippery part, and he shot down to the water like a streak of lightning! He didn't grin any more, poor Brer Bear—he gave a howl that could be heard a mile away, and he hit the water—kerplunkity-plunk—just like a chimney falling!

And when he came up out of the water, what did Brer Rabbit and Brer Terrapin and Mr. Mud Turtle see? They saw that Brer Bear's tail had gone—he hadn't got more than a little dob left, and a mighty queer creature he looked! When he had slid down that rock, his tail had broken off, smick, smack, smoove—and there he was, without a tail!

Brer Bear shot off up the road, howling, and Brer Rabbit shouted out: "Heyo, Brer Bear! I can lend you some ointment if you want it!"

But Brer Bear didn't even look back! And since that day bears have had no tails to speak of—just little dobs without a wag in them!

Brer Fox's New House

IT HAPPENED ONCE that old Brer Fox got himself a fine new house. My, wasn't he proud of it too! He called it Bushy Villa, after his tail, and he got Mrs. Bear to make him some blue curtains.

Now Brer Rabbit had wanted the house for himself, and he was in a great rage when he found that Brer Fox had walked in and taken it.

He set off to the house and knocked at the door, blim-blam!

"Who's there?" called Brer Fox.

"Brer Rabbit!" said Brer Rabbit.

"Come right in, Brer Rabbit!" sang out Brer Fox. But Brer Rabbit knew better than that. He just stood out there on the doorstep and shouted.

"Brer Fox! I'd like this house myself. I've come to offer you a good price for it."

"Then you can think again, Brer Rabbit," said Brer Fox, pleased to find that he had got something that Brer Rabbit wanted. "I'm in this house and here I stay! Good morning to you!"

Brer Rabbit was in a fine rage. He set off home, thinking with all his brains—and he had a good many. As he went along, head down and ears up, who should he meet but Brer Terrapin, the same old one-and-sixpence!

"How-do, Brer Rabbit," yelled out Brer Terrapin. "Look where you're going!"

"How-do, Brer Terrapin!" said Brer Rabbit, stopping and grinning at his old friend. "Why, Brer Terrapin, you are just the person I want to see. I've got a plan."

Brer Terrapin walked along by Brer Rabbit, listening to his plan of getting Brer Fox out of the house.

"You see, Brer Terrapin, if I can frighten him away, he'll sell it to me," said Brer Rabbit. "Now what about me sitting up on the roof and hanging things down the chimney when Brer Fox is sitting there reading his paper? Don't you think that would give him a shock?"

"I should just think it would!" said Brer Terrapin. "And what about me sitting there with him that evening and pretending I can't see anything coming down the chimney? That would be funnier still."

So it was arranged that Brer Terrapin should drop in at Brer Fox's house the next evening, and that Brer Rabbit should sit up on the roof with a fishing-line and drop things down on the end of the string.

"I'll tie my old tin teapot on first," giggled Brer Rabbit. "Then I'll tie an old boot. And then I'll tie Brer Fox's own hat. I'll slip into the hall and get it, once you are sitting talking to him, Brer Terrapin. That will give him a shock all right!"

Well, the next evening Brer Terrapin ambled along to Brer Fox's, and knocked at the door, blim, blam! Brer Fox was pleased to see him and asked him in.

"I've got a good fire, Brer Terrapin," he said. "Come along in and warm your toes."

As soon as they were safely in the parlour, Brer Rabbit crept into the hall and took Brer Fox's best hat. Then, with his old tin teapot under his arm, and a dirty old boot and his fishing-line in his pocket, he climbed quietly up to the roof. He sat beside the chimney and cocked his ear up to hear what Brer Terrapin was saying to Brer Fox.

"You know, Brer Fox," Brer Terrapin was saying, "this house feels kind of funny to me. I guess I wouldn't like to live in it myself!"

"Pooh!" said Brer Fox; "you don't know what you are talking about, Brer Terrapin. This house is just an ordinary, comfortable place, with nothing queer about it at all."

"There'll be something queer mighty soon!" said Brer Rabbit to himself, and he tied the tin teapot on to the end of his line. He dropped the line carefully down the chimney, and the teapot rattled against the bricks all the way down, clitter-clatter, clitter-clatter!

Brer Fox heard the noise and looked surprised. Brer Terrapin sucked at his old pipe and pretended to hear nothing at all. Down the chimney came the tin teapot and swung over the flames, just near Brer Fox's nose.

Brer Fox stared as if he couldn't believe his eyes. A teapot! Down the chimney! Hanging there as if by magic! Now what could be the meaning of that?

He spoke to Brer Terrapin in a low voice. "Brer Terrapin! What do you suppose that tin teapot is doing in my chimney?"

Brer Terrapin turned and stared at Brer Fox as if he were greatly surprised. "Tin teapot!" he said. "What are you talking about, Brer Fox? Tin teapot, indeed! You'll be telling me it's dancing a jig next!"

Brer Rabbit, up on the roof, grinned when he heard that. He at once jerked his line and the teapot jumped up and down for all the world as if it were dancing a jig. Brer Fox clutched his whiskers and groaned.

"It *is* dancing a jig!" he said. "Brer Terrapin, do just look! Surely you can see a tin teapot dancing about in the chimney?"

Brer Terrapin turned towards the chimney and shut his eyes. "No," he said truthfully, "I can't see any teapot there, Brer Fox. Are you playing a joke on me?"

The teapot disappeared, and Brer Fox heaved a sigh. "Well, it's gone now," he said. "What a peculiar thing! A teapot in my chimney, and you don't see it, Brer Terrapin!"

"Don't you tell that kind of story to an old chap like me," said Brer Terrapin, settling himself more comfortably in his chair. "It's no good you expecting me to believe tales of teapots, Brer Fox, nor of anything else either!"

Slither-slither-slosh! Down the chimney came the old boot, tied tightly to the end of the string! Brer Fox leapt up from his chair in fright and stared at it.

"There's a boot now!" he cried. "Can't you see it, Brer Terrapin?"

"No, that I can't," said Brer Terrapin, looking at the chimney with his eyes shut again. "I can't see a thing. Do sit down, Brer Fox, and don't keep jumping and shouting. You make me quite uncomfortable."

"Well, I'm not used to teapots and boots jigging in my chimney-place," said Brer Fox fiercely. "You said there was something funny about this house, Brer Terrapin, and so there is. I don't like it."

"Sit down, Brer Fox, sit down," begged Brer Terrapin, sucking at his pipe. "How can a man enjoy his pipe when you keep shouting about teapots and boots I can't see? Don't be silly."

The boot disappeared. Brer Fox stared at the chimney-place for a while and then sat down on the edge of his seat, watching the chimney. No sooner had he sat down than the boot slithered down again, and poor Brer Fox shot out of his seat, fell over Brer Terrapin, and sat down heavily on the floor.

Brer Terrapin wanted to laugh but he dared not. "Goodness gracious, Brer Fox, what are you doing now?" he said. "Something else come down the chimney? Well, well, well, I don't know what you wanted to buy this house for! I heard that Brer Rabbit wanted it, and I'm sure I don't know why you didn't let him have it."

"I don't know why either," groaned Brer Fox. "I'd sell it to him now, I know that!"

Brer Rabbit grinned in delight. He tied the fine new hat on to the end of his line, and let that down the chimney too. Swish-swish-swish it came, sweeping all the soot on to the brim as it went, so that Brer Fox's fine hat looked very sorry for itself when at last it appeared in the fireplace.

Brer Fox stared in horror. "Look, Brer Terrapin, look!" he said. "There's my new hat! Oh my, oh my, it's my new hat! I can't bear it! I can't bear it!"

Brer Rabbit leant right over the chimney and nearly burst himself with laughing. But he didn't know what was going to happen next! Brer Fox was so wild at seeing his beautiful new hat dancing in the chimney covered with soot that he suddenly made a dart at it and caught hold of it! He pulled hard—and Brer Rabbit overbalanced and fell right into the chimney himself! Down he went, slither-swish, and landed in the hearth. He gave a great yell when he sat on the flames, and shot off like a bullet out of a gun!

Even Brer Terrapin got a shock that time, and he ran out of the house faster than any terrapin ran before. Brer Fox was scared too, for he wondered what was coming down the chimney *this* time! But when he saw it was Brer Rabbit, he was after him like lightning.

And Brer Rabbit lost a few hairs out of his tail that night, he was so nearly caught. He didn't get Brer Fox's house after all, and how he shook his fist when Brer Fox met him and called after him, "Hie! Sweep! Would you like to come and do my chimneys for me?"

Aha, Brer Rabbit, you didn't win that time!

Brer Fox and Mr. Jack Sparrow

ONE DAY, after he had been tricked by old Brer Terrapin, Brer Rabbit was sitting down in the woods trying to puzzle out how he might get even with Brer Terrapin. He felt mighty lonesome and he felt mighty mad, Brer Rabbit did.

There he sat, all by himself, and thought and thought, and by and by he jumped up and shouted:

"Well, I'll eat my tail if I can't outdo old Brer Fox—and Brer Terrapin—and the whole lot of them! I'll show Miss Meadows and the girls that I'm the best of the lot! I'll make Brer Fox come a-crawling round me, oh yes, I will!"

There was a little Jack Sparrow up in the tree, and he heard what Brer Rabbit said.

"I'm going to tell Brer Fox what you said," sang out the Jack Sparrow. "I'm going to tell Brer Fox what you said! Chick-a-biddy-wind-a-blowing-acorns-falling! I'm going to tell Brer Fox!"

Well, when Brer Rabbit heard that Jack Sparrow was going to tell tales of him, he was mighty mad and mighty wild. He just didn't want Brer Fox or anybody to know what he had been planning. He sat and thought for a moment.

"The one that sees Brer Fox first will be the one he listens to!" said Brer Rabbit with a grin. "I'm off home and on the way I'll call on Brer Fox and tell him just a few things!"

He hadn't gone far when who should come round the corner but old Brer Fox himself.

"Heyo, Brer Fox!" said Brer Rabbit. "Now then, just you tell me what all this fuss is between you and me?"

"What fuss?" said Brer Fox in surprise.

"Oh, I hear tell you're going to send me packing, and grab

my family and burn my house down!" said Brer Rabbit, looking mighty fierce.

Then Brer Fox got mad and shouted, "Who's been telling you all those make-ups?"

"Oh, I'm not telling you that," said Brer Rabbit.

"You just go right on and tell me who said that!" said Brer Fox. "Go on, now, Brer Rabbit—you tell me! Someone's been making trouble between you and me, sure enough, and I didn't know a thing about it!"

"Well, I didn't mean to tell you," said Brer Rabbit, "but it was that meddling Jack Sparrow I heard saying all this. And, Brer Fox, when I heard him say you were going to send me off and grab my family, and burn my house down, I just lost my temper, so I did, and I got so mad that I stamped around and knocked down a few trees!"

Brer Fox gaped to hear this and got a bit further away from Brer Rabbit.

"I think I'll be going home," he said. And off he went.

But bless us all, he hadn't gone far before Jack Sparrow flipped down on a bush by the side of the road and shouted out:

"Brer Fox! Oh, Brer Fox! Brer Fox!"

Brer Fox cantered on as if he didn't hear Jack Sparrow. Then Jack Sparrow began to yell again:

"Brer Fox! Oh, Brer Fox! Hold on, Brer Fox! I've got some news for you. Wait, Brer Fox! I'll tell you something that will astonish you!"

Of course, Jack Sparrow didn't know that Brer Fox had seen Brer Rabbit first, and he didn't guess all that Brer Rabbit had told Brer Fox about him. But Brer Fox knew all right, and he went on his way, pretending that he didn't either see or hear Jack Sparrow. He meant to play a little trick on him!

By and by Brer Fox lay down by the roadside, and kind of stretched himself, and yawned as if he meant to take a nap. The tattling Jack Sparrow flew along and kept on calling Brer Fox, but Brer Fox didn't answer a word. He was pretending he was deaf.

Then the little Jack Sparrow flew down to the ground and fluttered about in the grass. Brer Fox looked up and saw him there, and when the little tale-teller saw him looking, he shouted and shouted:

"I've got something to tell you, Brer Fox! I've got something to tell you!"

"Get on my tail, little Jack Sparrow," said Brer Fox, "because I'm deaf in one ear and I can't hear out of the other. Get on my tail!"

Then the little bird hopped up on Brer Fox's tail.

"Get on my back, little Jack Sparrow," said Brer Fox, "because I'm deaf in one ear and I can't hear out of the other!"

Then the little bird hopped on to his back.

"Hop on my head, little Jack Sparrow," said Brer Fox, "because I'm deaf in both ears."

Up hopped the little bird.

"Hop on my tooth, little Jack Sparrow," said Brer Fox, "because I'm deaf in one ear and I can't hear out of the other."

The little taming bird hopped on to Brer Fox's tooth—and then—and then—Brer Fox opened his mouth wide—and when he shut it again the tattling Jack Sparrow was gone!

And when Brer Rabbit came along there the next day and found a few little feathers, he shook his wicked head and said: "All tale-tellers come to a bad end! I could have told Jack Sparrow that—only he didn't ask me!"

Brer Rabbit and the Butter

IT HAPPENED ONCE that the creatures made a lot of very fine butter, and they agreed to put it into a cool shed, and share it between them.

But Brer Rabbit wasn't to have any at all, because he was such a rascal. Brer Fox winked all round and said, "That will teach old Brer Rabbit to stop tricking us! When he doesn't get his butter, he'll be sorry!"

Now Brer Rabbit was as angry as a dozen wildcats when he heard that he wasn't to share in the butter. He sat in his house and he scratched first one ear and then the other, trying to think of some way he could get that butter.

Well, he guessed if he went along that way at night he'd get that butter all right! So each night Brer Rabbit slid between the trees and came to the shed where the butter was kept. He opened the door, went to the butter-pail and scooped out a nice pat of butter. Then off he went as quietly as he had come.

Now when the creatures found their butter going every night, they knew there was a thief somewhere. And they guessed it was their old friend, Brer Rabbit!

"We'll set a trap for him!" said Brer Fox, grinning. "That's what we'll do. We'll spread the shed-floor with black soot, and old Brer Rabbit won't see it in the dark! It will get on to his shoes, and in the morning we'll see a sooty track leading back to his house—then we'll all know who the thief is!"

Well, every one thought that was a fine idea, and Brer Wolf, he swept his chimney, put the soot into a sack and took it along to the butter-shed. He spread the floor with the soot and went away.

Now that night along came Brer Rabbit as usual for his pat of butter. It was dark and he couldn't see the soot—but he could smell it all right! Oh yes, Brer Rabbit knew the smell of fresh soot, and he stood there in the shed and sniffed hard.

"Soot on the floor!" said Brer Rabbit, and he grinned to himself. "Put there to catch me! Ha, they think they'll see my sooty footsteps leading to my house—and they'll come and say I steal the butter. No, no, Brer Fox, you can't trick me so easily as that!"

Brer Rabbit took his pat of butter and skipped out on his sooty feet. He walked as heavily as he could to a tree. Then he took off his sooty shoes and pressed them hard against the tree-trunk so that it looked for all the world as if some one had been walking up there!

Then Brer Rabbit skipped home in his bare feet, carrying the shoes, as happy as a jay-bird!

The next morning the creatures were excited to see the sooty footmarks. They all followed them till they came to the tree, and they were *most* astonished to see the footprints going up the trunk!

"Queer!" said Brer Fox, looking hard at them.

"The thief must live up in this tree," said Brer Wolf, peering up. "But only Cousin Wildcat lives in trees."

"Well, one of us must go up and see who lives here," said

Brer Bear. "Brer Turkey-Buzzard, you fly up and see what you can find."

So Brer Turkey-Buzzard flew up, but though he spent hours looking into every hole and along every branch, he simply could *not* find the thief!

Well, the next night Brer Rabbit skipped along for his butter again, and walked hard on the soot. When he left the shed he walked along to the bank of the river. Then he took off his shoes and ran along home in his bare feet once more.

The next day all the animals found the sooty footprints once again, and followed them in glee. This time they would surely find the thief!

"The footmarks stop just here!" said Brer Fox in astonishment, and he pointed to the bank of the river. "Maybe Brer Terrapin, or his Uncle Mud-Turtle, is the thief!"

"Indeed we're not!" said Brer Terrapin, who had come along with the others. "Last night we were at a party at Mr. Benjamin Ram's, as he'll tell you. We didn't go near the butter-shed!"

"Well, it's a strange thing," said Brer Wolf, puzzled. "First those footsteps lead us to a tree—and now they lead us to a river!"

The next night Brer Rabbit fetched his butter and danced off in his sooty shoes. He skipped along till he came to the middle of a field, then he took off his shoes and ran home.

And when the creatures found the footmarks stopping in the middle of the field, they looked at one another in amazement.

"Well, the thief must have wings!" said Brer Fox. "He couldn't just disappear like that! I wonder if it's Brer Turkey-Buzzard."

"No, it isn't," said Brer Turkey-Buzzard indignantly. "I was away at my uncle's all last night, as he will tell you."

Now just then along came old Brer Rabbit, and he saw all the animals looking puzzled and talking to one another. So he skipped up and said how-do to them.

"What's puzzling you?" he asked. "You tell me, and I'll help you!"

So they told him about the missing butter, and how they couldn't make out who the thief was because one time he walked up a tree, and another time he went into the river, and the third time he just disappeared in the middle of a field!

"You let *me* keep your butter for you in *my* shed and it'll be all right!" said Brer Rabbit. "I guess no thief will dare to come around tricking me! You let me take care of the butter!"

"Well, we'll pay you a pat of butter each day if you'll keep the thief away," said Brer Fox. "But if you don't, you won't get any butter, Brer Rabbit!"

"You trust me to keep the thief away!" grinned old Brer Rabbit. "I won't need any soot to catch him either! The thief's afraid of me! I'm fierce, I am, and no one will take your butter!"

So the butter was moved to Brer Rabbit's shed, and the creatures gave him a large piece of it every day for keeping it safe. No thief came near it, of course, so the creatures were very pleased.

"Oh, Brer Rabbit's a mighty fierce fellow!" they said to each other. "No thief dares to get our butter now!"

And they wondered why old Brer Rabbit grinned when he heard them. He's a rascal, isn't he?

Brer Rabbit Gets Brer Bear

ONE TIME WHEN Brer Rabbit was going loping home from a party up at Miss Meadows', who should he come across but old Brer Bear! Of course, after the wicked way that Brer Rabbit had tricked Brer Bear in Brer Fox's pea-patch, there weren't very good feelings between the two of them.

But Brer Rabbit, he was as cheeky as ever, and he shouted out: "Heyo, Brer Bear! How are you getting along? I haven't seen you for a week of Sundays! How is everybody down at your house?"

Well, Brer Bear, he meant to grab Brer Rabbit this time, so he answered mighty politely.

"Fine, thank you, Brer Rabbit, fine. And how's yourself?"

"Oh, I've got a thorn in my paw," said Brer Rabbit, "but my old woman will take that out for me as soon as I get home."

"Let me see it," said Brer Bear—and as soon as Brer Rabbit stretched out his paw, Brer Bear grabbed it and held on to it as if he couldn't let go.

"You come along home with me and I'll get the thorn out for you, Brer Rabbit," said Brer Bear, talking in a friendly voice, but snapping his jaws all the same.

Brer Rabbit didn't like the look of things at all. But he didn't give his feelings away, he just went on walking beside old Brer Bear, who was holding his paw hard enough to squash it to bits.

"I've been busy this last month, Brer Bear," said Brer Rabbit, talking just as friendly as Brer Bear. "I've been cleaning up a big bit of new ground I've got."

"Well, you'll like a bit of a rest now, I expect," said Brer Bear, with a nasty sort of grin.

"And do you know what I found in my new ground, Brer Bear?" said Brer Rabbit. "I came across one of these old, old bee-trees. It was a tree that was hollow from the bottom to the top, and the bees had found it and put their nest there, and the honey was just oozing out of it!"

"Is that so?" said Brer Bear, in a disbelieving sort of manner.

"That surely is so," said Brer Rabbit, "and if you don't mind just coming along with me, Brer Bear, you'll get enough honey to last you and your family till the middle of next month!"

"Well, I believe I'll go along," said Brer Bear, who thought

maybe there might be a speck of truth in Brer Rabbit's tale—and if there wasn't, well, Brer Rabbit would be sorry!

And with that they set out for Brer Rabbit's new patch of ground, which wasn't very far. They got there after a while, and old Brer Bear, he put his nose up into the air and said he could smell the honey all right!

They got to a big hollow tree, and sure enough, there were bees coming in and out, humming mighty loud.

"Yes, that honey smells good," said Brer Bear, and his mouth began to water.

Brer Rabbit bent his head down to a hole at the bottom of the tree.

"I can see the honeycomb," he said. "My, this is a mighty fine bee-tree, Brer Bear."

"I can hear the bees a-zooming," said Brer Bear, who was longing to get at the honey and yet didn't want to let go Brer Rabbit's paw.

"Well, what about it?" said Brer Rabbit. "Will you do the climbing, Brer Bear, and I'll do the rushing round? You climb up to the hole at the top there, and I'll take this pine-pole and push the honey up where you can get it."

Well, that sounded pretty good to old Brer Bear, so he climbed up the tree and jammed his head in at the hole. Sure enough Brer Rabbit grabbed the pine-pole and put it in the little hole at the bottom—but he didn't push the honeycomb up to Brer Bear! No, he just stirred up those bees till they were mad enough to sting for a year! And they all swarmed up the tree to get out of the hole there.

But old Brer Bear's head was jammed in there, waiting for the honey, and those bees, they couldn't get out at all. So they just swarmed on to Brer Bear's head and stung him hard.

And before he could get his head out it was all swelled up, and he couldn't take it out at all! So there he swung, growling and grunting, his head bigger than a dinner-pot, whilst Brer Rabbit danced round and sang:

> *"Trees stand high and honey's mighty good,*
> *Watch those bees a-stinging in the wood!"*

Then Brer Bear growled more than ever and tried to jerk out his head, but it wasn't a bit of good. He had to wait till the swelling went down before he could take his head away—and by that time Brer Rabbit was gone!

Brer Rabbit and the Alligator

ONE TIME BRER RABBIT went down to the river to catch some fish for breakfast. He saw something long and brown lying in the mud, and he thought it was a big log. He was pleased, and he ran up to it.

"Here's a fine big log to fish from. I'll stand on it to catch the fish."

So Brer Rabbit jumped on to the log. He got ready his line. He fixed his hook. As he was doing this the log moved.

Brer Rabbit was mighty scared and he squealed out, "Oh, my goodness!" He looked down—and his eyes nearly dropped out of his head when he saw that what he had thought was a log was really a big alligator.

Mr. Alligator swam away with Brer Rabbit on his back. He flicked his tail round and knocked Brer Rabbit between his two front paws. He grinned very wide indeed, and sniffed at Brer Rabbit with his nose.

"I'll take you to my home," said Mr. Alligator. "I've got seven eggs there, and when they hatch into baby alligators they shall have you for their dinner."

Mr. Alligator swam towards the hole in the bank where he lived. He crawled into the hole and carried Brer Rabbit in with him. Brer Rabbit was mighty scared.

"I've a good mind to eat you myself," said Mr. Alligator,

looking at Brer Rabbit, who was plump and not at all bony. "Yes, so I have, Brer Rabbit."

"Please, Mr. Alligator, leave me here to look after your eggs for you," said Brer Rabbit. "I'm a good nurse, I am. I can look after your eggs whilst you go a-swimming down the river, and you'll know they're safe. You let me nurse your eggs."

Mr. Alligator flicked his big tail and said, "I'll try you for one day. If you mind my eggs well, I'll not eat you."

Then the old alligator went away and left Brer Rabbit to mind his eggs. He had got to get something for his breakfast. Brer Rabbit sat down beside the eggs. He couldn't get out of the hole, and he was so scared that he shivered like a jelly.

Brer Rabbit waited and waited for Mr. Alligator to come back. By and by he got hungry. He waited and he waited. He minded the eggs and turned them over with his paw. Soon he felt so hungry that he could hardly hold up his head. He sucked his paw. He waited and he waited. The alligator didn't come. He had gone a long way down the river. Brer Rabbit sucked his other paw and waited and waited. Still the alligator didn't come.

Then Brer Rabbit stood up. "Huh!" said he, "I'm not going to starve myself when there's plenty of food under my nose."

He snatched up one of the seven alligator eggs, made a hole in it, and sucked it. It was a big egg and it made a good meal. Brer Rabbit threw the egg-shell right to the back of the hole. He rubbed his middle and grinned.

"Hoo! I feel better now. I don't know what I'm going to tell the old alligator when he comes back, but I don't care. I feel good and I'm not going to worry about any old alligator. I'll think of something when he comes."

Brer Rabbit lay down. He curled himself up on the eggs. He shut his eyes and slept soundly. By and by, when night was almost come, Mr. Alligator came back. He shouted loudly to Brer Rabbit:

"Hey, Brer Rabbit! How can you mind my eggs when you've gone to sleep?"

Brer Rabbit sat up at once. "My eyes have gone to sleep, but my ears are wide awake," he said.

Mr. Alligator flicked his tail and said, "Where are my eggs?"

Brer Rabbit felt a bit scared. Suppose Mr. Alligator counted his eggs?

"They're all here, Mr. Alligator," he said. "Wait—let me count them—one, two, three, four, five, six, seven. Yes, they're all here, Mr. Alligator."

Mr. Alligator was pleased. He opened his mouth wide and grinned. "You've minded them well, Brer Rabbit," he said. "Bring each one out for me to see. I want to count them."

Brer Rabbit felt mighty scared at this. He carried one egg out to Mr. Alligator, who sniffed it. Brer Rabbit took it back and brought out the second. Then he took that back and brought out the third—then the fourth—then the fifth—and then the sixth, which was the last one.

After that Brer Rabbit stopped, and didn't know what to do. Mr. Alligator yelled out, "Fetch me the seventh one."

Well, Brer Rabbit, he just picked up the first one again and hurried out with that. Mr. Alligator, he didn't know it was the same egg he had seen the first time, and he just sniffed at it and told Brer Rabbit to take it back.

"You've minded them well," he said to Brer Rabbit. "You can mind them again tomorrow."

So the next day Mr. Alligator went off again and left Brer Rabbit minding his eggs. And Brer Rabbit felt so mighty hungry that he ate another one. That night when Mr. Alligator came home, Brer Rabbit took him out the five eggs and then took the first two out again, to make seven—and Mr. Alligator, he didn't know anything was wrong at all.

Well, every day Brer Rabbit ate an egg belonging to Mr. Alligator, and each night he carried the same eggs out so that

Mr. Alligator would think there were seven. And at last there was only one egg left.

"I'll have to carry it out seven times," grinned Brer Rabbit to himself, when he heard Mr. Alligator coming home.

"Where are my eggs, Brer Rabbit?" called Mr. Alligator.

"They're all here, Mr. Alligator," Brer Rabbit shouted out from the hole in the bank.

"I met Brer Fox today, Brer Rabbit," said Mr. Alligator, "and he told me you are mighty fond of eggs. So this time I think I'll mark each egg as you bring it, and then I'll know for certain you haven't been eating *my* eggs, Brer Rabbit. Ha, you may be a clever man, Brer Rabbit, but Mr. Alligator is just as smart as you. And I tell you this, if so much as one of my eggs is missing I'll have you for my supper tonight, sure as I've got a tail."

Brer Rabbit shook in his shoes. He felt more scared than he had ever been in his life. But he put on a bold face and shouted back to Mr. Alligator:

"That's right, Mr. Alligator! You mark your eggs and then you'll know. And don't you listen to any tales from Brer Fox— he's a scamp and I'd just like to tell him so."

"Bring out the first egg and let me mark it," shouted Mr. Alligator.

So Brer Rabbit brought out the first and only egg. Mr. Alligator rubbed some mud on it to mark it. He gave it back to Brer Rabbit. "Now bring out the next," he said.

Brer Rabbit ran back to the hole. He rubbed off the mud on the egg, made it quite clean, and took it out again to Mr. Alligator. "Number two egg," he said.

Mr. Alligator took it and made a mark on it with mud again. He didn't know it was the same egg, because Brer Rabbit had rubbed it clean. "Bring out the third egg," he said.

So Brer Rabbit ran back again, rubbed the egg clean, and took it out for the third time to Mr. Alligator. "Number three egg," he said.

Well, that rascal of a Brer Rabbit brought the same old egg out seven times to Mr. Alligator, and each time Mr. Alligator marked it with mud and Brer Rabbit rubbed it off in the hole. And when Mr. Alligator had marked the egg seven times, and thought it was the seventh egg, he was very pleased.

"Yes, Brer Rabbit, you've minded them well," he said. "There are my seven eggs all perfect. I won't eat you for supper."

"Mr. Alligator," said Brer Rabbit, popping his head out of the hole, "I can hear Brer Fox a-barking away in the woods yonder. Will you give me leave to go and tell him what I think of him? He's no business to be telling you stories about me, when I'm doing my duty and minding your eggs so well."

"Yes, you go and tell him, Brer Rabbit," said Mr. Alligator. "You go and tell him. But mind you're back before daybreak to nurse my eggs again. I'll go in and look after them whilst you're gone."

Brer Rabbit thanked Mr. Alligator kindly and hopped out of the hole. He jumped on to Mr. Alligator's back and ran lightly across it to the bank. He stood there and watched Mr. Alligator go in to his hole to mind his eggs. And then he didn't wait any more, because he heard a loud bellow and a great scrambling round in the hole, and knew Mr. Alligator had found he had only one egg left.

My, you couldn't see Brer Rabbit for dust then. He tore off at top speed, and he didn't go down to the river again till he heard that Mr. Alligator had gone away for good. He didn't think Mr. Alligator would ask him to mind his eggs for him again.

Brer Rabbit and Brer Bear

ONE SUMMER BRER FOX said to himself that he'd better hurry up and plant his pea-patch. So he got his spade, dug up his ground and planted out his peas.

Old Brer Rabbit came by when he was planting them, and when he thought of juicy ripe peas he winked his eye at his children and sang:

> "Ti-yi! Tungalees!
> I'll eat his peas, I'll pick his peas!
> I'll get each pod and give it a squeeze,
> Ti-yi! What juicy peas!"

Sure enough when the peas began to ripen, Brer Fox found that someone had been down in the pea-patch, eating his peas, and he felt mighty mad. He guessed he knew who the someone was, but old Brer Rabbit was so smart that Brer Fox really didn't know how to catch him.

By and by, one day Brer Fox took a walk all round his pea-patch and it wasn't long before he found a hole in the fence that had been rubbed quite smooth with somebody passing in and out.

"Look at that!" said Brer Fox to himself. "Right there is where the thief comes in and out. This is where I'll set a trap!"

He saw a young hickory-tree growing near by. He took a piece of string and tied one end to the top of the tree. He pulled the string and the tree bent half over. Then Brer Fox made a loop-knot at the other end of the string and fixed it neatly round the hole in the fence, keeping it in place with a stick. As soon as anyone crept in through the hole, the string would tighten round him, and the hickory tree would jerk up straight, taking the robber with it, swinging on the end of the string. My, that would be a fine scare for old Brer Rabbit, next time he came lolloping in through the hole!

Next morning, when old Brer Rabbit came slipping along and crept through the hole, the loop-knot caught him tightly, the hickory flew up straight, and there was Brer Rabbit swinging between the earth and the sky!

There he swung, afraid of falling, and yet afraid of not falling—for he didn't know what old Brer Fox would say when he came along and found him there!

While he was making up a tale to tell to Brer Fox when he came, he heard a lumbering noise down the road, and presently along came Brer Bear. Brer Rabbit hailed him.

"Heyo, Brer Bear!"

Brer Bear looked about in surprise, and by and by he saw Brer Rabbit swinging from the tree.

"Heyo, Brer Rabbit!" he shouted. "How are you this morning?"

"Much obliged to you, I'm just middling, Brer Bear," said Brer Rabbit.

"What are you doing up there?" asked Brer Bear in surprise.

"Huh, I'm making a shilling a minute up here," said Brer Rabbit.

"How's that?" asked Brer Bear, still more surprised.

"I'm up here frightening the crows out of Brer Fox's pea-patch," said Brer Rabbit. "Brer Fox pays me well for it."

"That's a fine job," said Brer Bear.

"Well, you come and have a turn at it," said Brer Rabbit, in a generous sort of voice. "You've a large family of children to work for, Brer Bear, and you'd make a fine scarecrow. I don't mind letting you have my job for a little while, just to do you a kindness."

"I'll take it, then," said Brer Bear, pleased. "How do I get up there, Brer Rabbit?"

"Bend down the tree," said Brer Rabbit. "And undo the string. It's quite easy."

Well, it wasn't long before Brer Rabbit was safely on the ground and old Brer Bear was swinging high up in Brer Rabbit's place. Then Brer Rabbit, he set out for Brer Fox's house, shouting:

"Brer Fox! Oh, Brer Fox! Come out here, Brer Fox, and I'll show you the man who's been stealing your peas!"

Brer Fox grabbed his walking-stick, and went running down to his pea-patch. When he got there, sure enough there was old

Brer Bear swinging in the trap!

"Oh, yes! You're caught!" said Brer Fox, and before Brer Bear could explain, Brer Rabbit jumped up and down shouting:

"Yes, there's the robber, Brer Fox! Whip him well, and don't you listen to any cheek from him!"

So, every time poor Brer Bear tried to explain how he came to be there, Brer Fox hit him a whack with his walking-stick, and made him squeal so that he couldn't say a word.

Whilst all this was going on, Brer Rabbit slipped off and got deep down into a mud-hole, for he knew Brer Bear would be after him as soon as he was free. He just left his big eyes sticking out of the mud-hole, for all the world like a frog peeping out.

By and by old Brer Bear came galloping down the road, looking everywhere for Brer Rabbit. When he got to the mud-hole he saw Brer Rabbit's eyes sticking out.

"Howdy, Brer Frog!" he said. "Have you seen Brer Rabbit anywhere?"

"He's just gone by," said Brer Rabbit, and Old Man Bear shot off down the road like a runaway horse, trying to catch up with Brer Rabbit.

And soon Brer Rabbit came out of the mud-hole, dried himself in the sun, brushed off the mud and went ambling home, whistling a little tune he knew:

> *"Ti-yi! Tungalees!*
> *I ate those peas, I picked those peas!*
> *I got each pod and gave it a squeeze,*
> *Ti-yi! What juicy peas!"*

Oh, wicked Brer Rabbit!

Brer Rabbit Catches Mice

NOW ONCE IT HAPPENED that Brer Fox stored away some fine carrots and juicy turnips in his little old shed. He was mighty pleased with them, for he had grown them himself, and meant to have them in his soup that winter.

And of course old Brer Rabbit smelt them out, and made up his mind to share those carrots and turnips—though he didn't mean to ask Brer Fox's permission!

So, each night, he crept to the door of the shed and opened it quietly. In he went, and nibbled a carrot here, and a turnip there.

Well, Brer Fox was angry to find his stores nibbled like that. He stared round his shed each morning and wondered who the thief was. He saw Brer Rabbit passing by in the distance and he called to him.

"Heyo, Brer Rabbit! Do you know anything about nibbled carrots?"

"Nibbled carrots!" said wicked Brer Rabbit, pretending to be surprised. "You don't mean to say you've got carrots in that shed that have been nibbled, Brer Fox?"

"That's just what I do mean to say," said Brer Fox, looking at Brer Rabbit in a very straight way.

"It must be that you've got mice there," said Brer Rabbit. "I'd put a few mouse-traps down, Brer Fox, that's what I'd do!"

And with that old Brer Rabbit went off whistling, telling himself he must remember to look out for a mouse-trap when he went a-nibbling that night!

But Brer Fox didn't put any traps down. No, he kept awake himself, and when he heard the door of his shed creaking he jumped out of his chair and crept out into the garden. He went to his shed, and flashed his lantern inside.

Brer Rabbit had heard him coming—but he couldn't get out of the door in time. So what did he do but turn his back to the wall of the shed, and stick his bobtail out through a hole in the wood. And there he was a-sitting when Brer Fox popped his head in at the door!

"Oh, Brer Rabbit! So I've just caught you, have I!" said Brer Fox.

"What do you mean, caught me?" asked Brer Rabbit, in a most astonished voice. "Here I've come to spend the whole night in your shed, to catch the mice that nibble your carrots— and you say you've caught me! That's not a nice way to repay a good deed, Brer Fox, and I'm really surprised at you."

Brer Fox looked astonished. "How are you catching mice for me?" he said.

"Why," said Brer Rabbit, "can't you see what I'm doing? I'm sitting here patiently with my tail out of a mouse-hole—and I'm waiting for a mouse to come along and nibble it—and then I'll pull in my tail like a shot and drag the mouse in at the hole for you!"

"I've never heard of that way of catching mice before," said Brer Fox, looking even more astonished. "Have you caught any yet?"

"Sh!" said Brer Rabbit. "I think I can feel one a-nibbling!"

Brer Fox shushed. But after a time Brer Rabbit sighed and shook his head.

"No," he said. "That one ran away. It's a pity my tail is so short, Brer Fox. Now, if I had a fine long one like yours, I'd catch twenty mice a night!"

"Would you really?" said Brer Fox, most interested. "Well, what about me poking my tail out through a hole and seeing if I can catch some?"

"Oh, I wouldn't bother to do that," said Brer Rabbit. "You wouldn't have the patience to sit still long enough for a mouse to come."

"Indeed I would," said Brer Fox. "I'm as patient as you are, any day."

Well, in the end Brer Fox found a good big mouse-hole and stuck his tail out of it so that it twitched on the ground outside the shed. And there he sat, whilst Brer Rabbit sat near him, his bobtail out too.

"Ha! I can feel one a-nibbling!" said Brer Rabbit suddenly. "Catch hold of my tail tightly, Mouse! Catch hold of it, I say!"

Brer Rabbit suddenly jerked his tail in and turned round to look at it as if he expected to see a mouse hanging on to the hairs. But there was nothing there, of course.

"Dear, dear!" said Brer Rabbit, sounding most disappointed. "What a pity! I made sure there was one that time. Keep still, Brer Fox, and see if he comes to your tail. And if you feel him a-nibbling, just call out, 'Catch hold of my tail, there, catch hold of my tail!'"

Now, just about daybreak, as Brer Rabbit very well knew, Brer Bear came along that way. And that was what Brer Rabbit was planning for. He listened and he listened for Brer Bear's footsteps, and pretty soon he heard them—clump-clump-clump.

He began to talk to Brer Fox so that he wouldn't hear them. "I can feel a mouse a-nibbling and a-gnawing!" he said. "Catch hold of my tail, there, catch hold of my tail! You shout too, Brer Fox, in case there's one at your tail too."

So Brer Fox shouted out, "Catch hold of my tail, there, catch hold of my tail!"

And just at that moment Brer Bear passed the shed, and saw Brer Fox's tail hanging out of the hole, and he heard him shouting, "Catch hold of my tail, there!"

"Funny thing!" said Brer Bear, sniffing at Brer Fox's tail, and touching it with his paw. "It looks like Brer Fox's tail. But what is it doing here? And why should I catch hold of it?"

When Brer Fox felt Brer Bear sniffing at his tail, he got very excited, because he really thought it was a mouse at last.

"Catch hold of my tail, there!" he shouted. "Catch hold of my tail!"

Brer Bear caught hold of his tail and held it tight. Brer Fox suddenly looked most astonished. This couldn't be a mouse!

"Something's got my tail!" he said to Brer Rabbit in a scared voice. Brer Rabbit ran to the door when he heard that welcome news, for he knew that Brer Fox couldn't get away to go after him then. He shot out of the door.

"I'll go and see what it is that's got your tail!" he shouted— and he took a look at Brer Bear and winked.

"Hold on for a bit, Brer Bear!" he said. "Hold on for a bit!" And with that he scampered away through the wood, lippitty-clippitty, and he didn't stop to laugh till he was safe at home with his door locked!

As for Brer Fox, there he had to stay in the shed till Brer Bear let go his tail. And what a quarrel there was then, to be sure, with Brer Fox calling Brer Bear names, and Brer Bear shouting at Brer Fox. They don't really know to this day that old Brer Rabbit played a mighty clever trick on them!

Brer Terrapin Shows His Strength

ONE NIGHT MISS MEADOWS and the girls gave a candy-party, and so many people came that they had to put the sugar for the candy into the big wash-pot, and make a big fire to boil it in the yard.

Brer Bear helped Miss Meadows to bring in the wood, Brer Fox made up the fire, Brer Wolf kept the dogs off, Brer Rabbit greased the bottom of the plates to keep the candy from sticking, and Brer Terrapin, he climbed up on a chair and said he'd see that the candy didn't boil over.

All the animals were there, and they were being mighty polite to one another, too, because Miss Meadows had put her foot down and said that if they came to her place they were to be friends with one another, or she'd know the reason why!

Well then, whilst they were all sitting out there in the yard, with the candy boiling and blubbering, they began to talk mighty biggitty.

"I'm the swiftest runner here!" said Brer Rabbit, greasing the plates. Brer Terrapin said nothing. He just rocked to and fro in his chair and watched the candy boiling.

"I'm the smartest here!" said Brer Fox, at once, throwing some wood on the fire. Brer Terrapin said nothing. He just went on rocking away.

"I'm the savagest!" said Brer Wolf, snarling at the dogs sniffing around. Brer Terrapin rocked and rocked in his chair.

"I'm the strongest!" said Brer Bear, carrying a great log up to the fire. Brer Terrapin rocked himself and rocked, and by and by he winked at the candy and said:

"Well, well, it looks as if an old shellyback like me isn't anyone at all in this crowd, yet here I am, and I'm the same man that showed Brer Rabbit he wasn't the swiftest runner—didn't I beat him in a race? And I'm the same man that can show Brer Bear he isn't the strongest!"

All the others stared at Brer Terrapin and laughed and shouted at him, for they knew that Brer Bear had the strength of ten. Miss Meadows came up just then, to stir the candy, and she asked them what they were laughing at.

"Old Man Terrapin says he's stronger than Brer Bear," they told her.

"How are you going to show you are stronger than Brer Bear?" asked Miss Meadows.

"Give me a good strong rope," said Brer Terrapin, "and let me get into a puddle of water, and then let Brer Bear see if he can pull me out! I tell you, he won't be able to budge me an inch!"

Then they all laughed again, and Brer Bear said: "We haven't got a rope."

"No," said Brer Terrapin, "and you haven't got the strength either, Brer Bear!" And then he rocked himself in his chair and watched the candy bubbling.

After a while Miss Meadows said she would lend them some rope, and whilst the candy was cooling on the plates, they could all go to the pond and see if Brer Terrapin was as strong as he made out. Brer Terrapin wasn't very big, and it sounded mighty funny to hear him boasting that he could out-pull Brer Bear.

Well, Miss Meadows gave them the rope and they all set out for the pond. When Brer Terrapin found the place he wanted, he took one end of the rope and gave the other end to Brer Bear.

"Now then, ladies and gentlemen," said Brer Terrapin, "you all go with Brer Bear up to those trees yonder and I'll stay here, and when you hear me shout, then is the time for Brer Bear to pull! You take care of your end of the rope," he said, "and I'll take care of mine!"

Then they all went up to the trees and left Brer Terrapin by the pond. When they were a good distance away Brer Terrapin dived down into the water and tied his end of the rope hard and fast to an old tree-stump down at the bottom of the pond. Then he swam up to the surface and gave a yell.

"Pull away, Brer Bear!" he shouted. "Pull away! I'm a-waiting to be pulled out of the water, I am! Pull away!"

Brer Bear wrapped the rope round his paw, winked at everybody and gave a big jerk at the rope. But Brer Terrapin didn't budge out of the water. He just sat there. Then Brer Bear put both paws to the rope and gave a bigger pull, but all the same, Brer Terrapin, didn't budge!

Then Brer Bear turned himself round and put the rope over his shoulders, and tried to walk off with Brer Terrapin but Brer Terrapin, he didn't move an inch out of the pond.

Then Brer Wolf took hold of the rope too and helped Brer Bear to pull, but it didn't make any difference at all. Brer Terrapin just sat in the pond and nobody could pull him out! Then everyone took hold of the rope and began to pull at the same time, panting and puffing like steam-engines going up a hill!

"Heyo there!" yelled Brer Terrapin. "Pull a bit harder, can't you? I don't think you're trying!"

Well, when they heard that, they dropped the rope and looked at one another in surprise. They just couldn't understand Brer Terrapin being so hard to pull out of the water.

As soon as Brer Terrapin saw the rope going slack, and knew they weren't pulling any more, he dived deep into the pond and undid his end of the rope from the tree-stump at the bottom. By the time everyone got up to the pond, Brer Terrapin was sitting in the edge of the water as natural as could be, holding the rope in his hands.

"Heyo, folks!" he said. "That last pull of yours was a mighty stiff one, and it would have got me out if it had been a bit stronger. You're mighty strong, Brer Bear, and you pull like a yoke of cart-horses, but I guess I can out-pull you any time!"

Well, Brer Bear didn't want to hear any more of this, so he said he expected the candy was ready for eating and they all set out to see. And when they got to the yard, sure enough the candy was ready. All the animals set to work to eat it, but this time there wasn't any biggitty talk!

As for Old Man Terrapin, he sat himself up in his chair again and rocked away merrily, eating the biggest pieces of candy he could see. And nobody, not even Brer Bear, dared to say he was greedy!

Brer Wolf is Still in Trouble

ONE TIME BRER RABBIT got Brer Wolf out of a mighty bad fix. It happened after Brer Wolf had had some of his hair scalded off him when Brer Rabbit's old woman spilt the kettle over him. Brer Wolf had to go away by himself to let his hair grow again, and he was gone so long that Brer Rabbit wondered what had happened to him.

"Well, I expect I can come down safely out of my steeple now," said Brer Rabbit, "and say how-do-you-do to folks."

So down he came, smartened himself up and then he set out for a walk to see who he could meet. He went to the cross-roads and chose a road to go down. Then off he galloped, enjoying stretching out his legs after being so long up in his steeple!

Well, he went on and on and he didn't meet anybody at all. Then he thought he heard something and he stopped to listen—and he heard somebody yelling.

"Oh my, oh my! Won't somebody come and help me?"

Brer Rabbit heard this and he listened hard. It wasn't long before he heard the somebody yelling out again. "Oh my, oh my! Please, won't somebody come and help me?"

Brer Rabbit, he put up his big ears and shouted back, "Who are you, anyhow, and what in the name of goodness is the matter?"

"Oh, please, somebody, do run here quickly!"

Brer Rabbit got ready to run, and yelled out, "Whereabouts are you, and how did you get there?"

"Oh, do please come quickly and help a poor miserable creature. I'm down here in the ditch under a big rock!"

Well, Brer Rabbit didn't quite know if it was a trick somebody was playing him, so he crept down into the ditch very quietly and looked in—and whoever do you suppose he saw there?

It was old Brer Wolf, that Brer Rabbit had scalded a week back. He was lying down in the ditch, and bless gracious, on top of him was a great big rock! It was so big that it looked as if it was squashing him flat—but he had strength enough, to yell and shout—and he yelled in such a miserable way that Brer Rabbit felt really sorry for him.

Brer Rabbit held his coat-tails up out of the way and slid down to the bottom of the ditch to see if he could help Brer Wolf.

When Brer Wolf saw him coming he spoke mighty politely to him.

"Oh, Brer Rabbit, kind sir, would you please help me in the removing of this rock?" he said.

"I expect I can help you all right," said Brer Rabbit.

"Well, Brer Rabbit, kind sir, just you hurry and do it!" groaned Brer Wolf.

So Brer Rabbit caught hold of the rock and pulled hard, and it wasn't long before he had it on the move, and pretty soon that rock rolled into the ditch-bottom and Brer Wolf was free!

Well, Brer Wolf stretched himself a bit to find out how many of his legs were broken—and it turned out that he wasn't hurt very much. Well, when he found this, Brer Wolf grinned and thought he could pounce on Brer Rabbit easily enough, and pay him out for all the tricks he had played on him. And no sooner did he think that than he grabbed Brer Rabbit by the back of the neck and the middle of the back!

Brer Rabbit kicked and squealed, but it wasn't any use, because the more he kicked the tighter Brer Wolf held him—and he squeezed him so hard that Brer Rabbit was afraid he was going to be choked.

"Well now, Brer Wolf!" said poor Brer Rabbit. "Is this the way you thank folks for saving your life?"

Brer Wolf gave a big grin and said, "I'll thank you kindly first, Brer Rabbit, and then I'll have you for dinner!"

"If you talk like that, Brer Wolf," said Brer Rabbit, "I'll never do you another good turn as long as I live!"

Brer Wolf grinned some more and said, "That you won't, Brer Rabbit, that you won't! You won't do me another good turn till you make me a good dinner!"

Well, Brer Rabbit thought hard for a moment and then he spoke solemnly to Brer Wolf. "Where I come from Brer Wolf, it's against the law for folks to kill any one that's done them a good turn, and I expect it's the law around here, too."

"I'm not so mighty sure about that," said Brer Wolf.

"Well," said Brer Rabbit, "what about us going to old Brer Terrapin, who's a mighty clever man, and see what he says about it?"

"I don't mind doing that," said Brer Wolf, "so long as I take you there in my mouth, Brer Rabbit!"

With that they set out for old Brer Terrapin's house, and when they got there Brer Wolf told his side of the story and Brer Rabbit told his. Old Brer Terrapin put on his spectacles, cleared his throat, and said:

"This seems all mixed up to me. I can't make head nor tail of it. Before I take any sides in the matter you'll just have to take me to see the place where Brer Wolf was when Brer Rabbit found him."

Well, they took Brer Terrapin to the ditch and they showed him the place where Brer Wolf had lain under the big rock. Old Brer Terrapin he walked round, he did, and poked at the place with the end of his stick.

By and by he shook his head and said:

"I do hate to put you folks to such trouble, but I'm afraid I'll have to see just how Brer Wolf was caught, and just how the rock was on top of him. I guess you'll both think I'm a troublesome chap, but I'll just have to get this right before I take sides."

117

Then Brer Wolf lay down where he was when Brer Rabbit found him, and the others rolled the rock on top of him so that Brer Terrapin could see everything just so. They rolled the rock on top of him, and there he was. Brer Terrapin walked all round and round and looked at him. Then he sat down, he did, and frowned as if he were thinking mighty hard and mighty deep.

By and by Brer Wolf began to grumble.

"Ooh, Brer Terrapin, this rock's getting mighty heavy!"

Brer Terrapin went on frowning and thinking. Brer Wolf began to wriggle under the rock and shouted, "Ooh, Brer Terrapin, this rock's squashing the breath out of me!"

Then Brer Terrapin sat up straight on his back legs, and spoke in a solemn voice.

"Brer Rabbit, listen to me. *You* were in the wrong, not Brer Wolf. You hadn't any business to go worrying around Brer Wolf when he wasn't bothering you. He was minding his own business and you should have been minding yours."

Brer Rabbit looked quite ashamed of himself. Brer Terrapin went on talking.

"When you were going along this road this morning, Brer Rabbit, you must surely have been going somewhere. If you *were* going somewhere, you'd better be going right now. Brer Wolf wasn't going anywhere this morning, and he isn't going anywhere now either! You found him under that rock, and under that rock you must leave him!"

And bless gracious, if those two creatures, Brer Rabbit and Brer Terrapin, didn't rush off and leave old Brer Wolf under that rock. Well, it served him right, didn't it?

Brer Fox Gets into Trouble

ONE TIME BRER RABBIT stole so many greens out of a garden that Mr. Man set a trap for him. And Brer Rabbit was so greedy that he walked right into the trap—spang!—before he knew it was there.

Well, it wasn't long before Mr. Man came around, and when he saw Brer Rabbit in the trap he smacked his hands together in joy and shouted: "You're a nice fellow, you are! You've been gobbling up my greens and now you're trying to run off with my trap! You're a mighty nice chap, that's what you are! But now that I've got you I'll just about settle a few things with you, Brer Rabbit, so I will!"

And with that Mr. Man went off to the bushes to find a handful of sticks to whip Brer Rabbit. Old Brer Rabbit said nothing, but he felt mighty lonesome and he sat there looking as if every minute was going to be the next.

Well, whilst Mr. Man was off looking for switches, who should come sauntering along but Brer Fox? When he saw Brer Rabbit tied up in the trap, he laughed and he danced all around him.

But Brer Rabbit burst out laughing himself, and he laughed fit to kill himself.

"What's the joke?" asked Brer Fox, in surprise.

"The joke is that Miss Meadows and the girls are having a party," said Brer Rabbit, "and they wanted me to go and I wouldn't. They said I must come, and I said no, and they said yes, and then by and by they tied me up here whilst they went off shopping for the party. They said I'd be here when they came back then, and they'd take me along to the party when they'd done their shopping."

"Well, it seems mighty funny to me that you don't want to go to a party," said Brer Fox.

"Ah, but you don't know my troubles," said Brer Rabbit, with a deep groan. "My children are ill and I want to go and buy some pills for them, and how can I, all tied up like this? You wouldn't feel like a party any more than I do, Brer Fox, if your children were ill and you wanted to go and buy pills for them and you couldn't."

"Well, I'll go and buy some pills for them," said Brer Fox.

"That's kind of you, Brer Fox," said Brer Rabbit. "You always were a good friend to me. But it would be kinder still if you'd just take my place here, and go down to the party with Miss Meadows and the girls instead of me, and let me go off shopping for my children."

"Well, I don't mind doing that," said Brer Fox. "I always did like pranking up at Miss Meadows'."

"Well, you undo me, then," said Brer Rabbit, "and I'll do you up in my place, Brer Fox." So Brer Fox undid Brer Rabbit and Brer Rabbit tied him up tightly in his place.

"Now I'm off to get some pills for my poor children," said Brer Rabbit. "You make my excuses nicely to Miss Meadows and the girls, Brer Fox."

Well, Brer Rabbit was hardly out of sight before up came Mr. Man with a handful of sticks from the bushes, all tied up into a switch to whip Brer Rabbit. And when he saw Brer Fox in the trap, he stopped and stared in surprise.

"Heyo!" said Mr. Man. "You've changed your colour, and you've got bigger, and you've grown a fine tail out at the back there! What kind of a creature are you, anyway!"

Brer Fox lay still and Mr. Man went on talking.

"It's a mighty big piece of luck for me," he said. "I catch the chap that nibbles my greens and at the same time I catch the fellow that steals my geese!"

And with that he began to hit poor Brer Fox with his hickory switch till it sounded like somebody beating a dusty carpet! Brer Fox, he jumped and he squealed and he howled, but Mr. Man hit out at him as if he were fighting a wasps' nest.

Well, by and by the hickory switch got worn out and Mr. Man set off to get some more. No sooner was he out of hearing than Brer Rabbit came along. He had been hiding in the bushes listening to the slaps and squeals.

"Heyo, Brer Fox," he said. "Has Miss Meadows come along yet to fetch you?"

"You wait till I fetch *you!*" said Brer Fox, in such a tearing rage that he pawed up the ground in big chunks.

"Well, it's mighty funny Miss Meadows hasn't been along yet," said Brer Rabbit. "I've been right down to the doctor's, and Miss Meadows ought to have been here by now. Well, Brer Fox, I hope you won't have to wait long. I must get along home."

Brer Rabbit turned as if he were about to go, and Brer Fox stopped tearing up the ground and began to speak politely.

"I'll thank you to turn me loose, Brer Rabbit," he said. "I'd be grateful to you if you would let me free. You've tied me up so tightly that it makes my head swim, and I don't think I'll be able to go to Miss Meadows' party if I feel so giddy. You turn me loose, Brer Rabbit, and I'll thank you."

Brer Rabbit sat down and yawned. He began to scratch his ear as if he were thinking hard about something.

"Well, Brer Fox, you surely look pretty bad," he said. "You look as if somebody's been combing your fur up the wrong way."

Brer Fox didn't say a word. But Brer Rabbit kept on talking.

"Brer Fox, there isn't any bad feeling between us, is there? Because, if you are feeling mad about anything, I'm going along home. I'm not staying here if you feel mad."

Brer Fox gritted his teeth, but he said: "Bless us all, Brer Rabbit, why should I be mad with you? No, there's no bad feeling between us. You untie me, Brer Rabbit, and you'll soon see I'm a good friend of yours."

So Brer Rabbit untied Brer Fox just as he heard Mr. Man a-whistling for his dogs—and Brer Fox shot off one way, and Brer Rabbit shot off the other.

But Brer Rabbit took mighty good care to keep out of Brer Fox's way for a long time after that!

Brer Rabbit is Nearly Caught

ONCE BRER RABBIT and Brer Terrapin sat talking and drinking lemonade in Brer Rabbit's kitchen. They were great friends, and my, how they laughed when they thought of all the times they had tricked Brer Fox!

But just as they were laughing, Brer Terrapin suddenly stopped, with his mouth wide open, staring hard at something.

"What's the matter, Brer Terrapin?" said Brer Rabbit, in surprise. "Have you got a bone stuck in your throat? Don't look like that!"

"Brer Rabbit, I saw Brer Fox and Brer Wolf pass by your window!" said Brer Terrapin, in a very scared voice. "I believe they're come to call on you. I don't like it, Brer Rabbit, I don't like it!"

"Quick!" said Brer Rabbit, as he heard a great banging at his front door. "Hide! Get under that saucepan, Brer Terrapin! And I'll get under this bucket!"

So in a twink the two were well hidden. There stood the pail and the saucepan upside down by the sink with the brushes and brooms—and Brer Terrapin and Brer Rabbit were trembling underneath!

"Blam-blam-blam!" Brer Fox knocked on the door again—and then, as there was no answer, he opened the door and looked round.

"Come on in, Brer Wolf," he said. "There's no one home. Brer Rabbit must have just gone out with some one. Look, they've been having lemonade, and they've left some in the jug! Let's finish it!"

"Right!" said Brer Wolf, pleased, for he was thirsty. "Then we'll hide under the bed and wait for Brer Rabbit to come back.

My, he'll be properly caught this time! He won't find that any of his tricks will help him now."

Brer Rabbit was boiling with rage under his bucket. To think that Brer Wolf and Brer Fox were drinking his lemonade! And goodness knew how long they would stay under the bed waiting for him!

"Glop-glop-glop!" Brer Wolf finished the lemonade, and then scrambled under the bed. He left his tail hanging out. Brer Fox got under the bed too. It was a tight squeeze, and he left *his* tail out as well!

"Hope he won't be long!" said Brer Wolf, who felt uncomfortable under the small bed.

"Sh!" said Brer Fox. "If you talk maybe he'll hear you, and then he'll be scared away."

The two of them lay still. Brer Rabbit and Brer Terrapin hardly dared to breathe. Brer Wolf suddenly sneezed and nearly blew the bed up into the air. Brer Fox was angry.

"Brer Wolf, can't you be quiet even for one moment?" he said.

"Don't talk to me like that, Brer Fox," said Brer Wolf, in a huff. "I couldn't help sneezing. Be quiet yourself!"

Whilst they were talking, Brer Rabbit and Brer Terrapin moved a little nearer the bed—but Brer Terrapin's saucepan made a little scraping noise. Brer Fox heard it.

"What was that?" he said. "Was that you making a noise again? Do be quiet, Brer Wolf—clanking like that!"

"Clanking! Who's clanking?" said Brer Wolf, annoyed. "What do you think I am? A wheel-barrow?"

Brer Rabbit and Brer Terrapin moved a little nearer. Brer Rabbit's bucket made a clanking noise on the stone floor. Brer Wolf heard it.

He turned to Brer Fox. "Ha!" he said. "*You* made a noise then—I heard you! Be quiet!"

"I didn't make any noise," said Brer Fox. " Sh! Is that some one coming?"

But it was only the wind blowing the curtains. Brer Rabbit and Brer Terrapin moved a little nearer, and the noise made Brer Wolf and Brer Fox jump.

"This house is full of noises," said Brer Fox. "I'd hate to live here!"

Now Brer Rabbit was so near Brer Wolf's tail that he could reach out a paw from under his bucket and pinch the long tail! Pinch!

"Ooo-ow!" cried Brer Wolf, in a rage. "What did you do that for, Brer Fox?"

"What did I do what for?" said Brer Fox, in astonishment, thinking that Brer Wolf must be mad. "I didn't do a thing!"

"You pinched my tail!" shouted Brer Wolf. "And now you've done it again!"

"I didn't!" said Brer Fox—and just then Brer Terrapin reached out a front paw and dug his claws into Brer Fox's bushy tail. "Ooooh! You've pinched *my* tail! Brer Wolf, don't behave so stupidly. Brer Rabbit will hear us!"

Brer Rabbit pinched Brer Wolf's tail again and Brer Terrapin dug his claws into Brer Fox's. The two creatures slapped at one another, and then began to fight under the bed. They tried to stand up—and over went the bed on top of Brer Terrapin's saucepan and Brer Rabbit's bucket!

They were scared, for they could not see what had happened. They tried to back away to the sink again under their bucket and saucepan, but they were covered with bedclothes, and couldn't see where they were going.

But Brer Wolf and Brer Fox saw the lumps under the bedclothes moving, and they stared in astonishment. "Look!" said Brer Wolf. "The bed's coming alive! Let's go!"

"It's something under the clothes!" said Brer Fox. He jerked off the blankets, and there he saw the bucket and the saucepan— and Brer Terrapin, trying to get away, put out all his feet, which showed under the saucepan's edge!

"Ow! It's a saucepan with feet!" squealed Brer Fox, in fright. "And look at that bucket! It's walking! It's alive too!"

Brer Wolf and Brer Fox gave one scared look at the jiggling saucepan and bucket and fled out of the door as fast as they could go.

Brer Terrapin tipped over his saucepan, and Brer Rabbit threw off his bucket. Then they both sat and laughed till Brer Terrapin nearly cracked his shell and Brer Rabbit nearly cracked his sides!

"I guess old Brer Wolf and old Brer Fox won't come *this* way again in a hurry," said Brer Rabbit, as he and Brer Terrapin put the bed into its place again. "My, you must have looked queer with your feet sticking out under the saucepan, Brer Terrapin! It's a mercy we got under so quickly—we'd have been somebody's dinner by now, if we hadn't!"

Brer Fox and Miss Goose

MISS GOOSE USED TO take in washing for everybody, and she made money at it, and got sleek and fat. She used to take the dirty linen down to the brook and bang it clean with her battling-stick, till it came white as snow.

Well, one day Brer Fox and Brer Rabbit were sitting talking to one another in the cotton-patch not far off the brook. As they chattered away, they heard a noise—*blim, blim, blim*!

"What's all that noise?" said Brer Fox.

"That's old Miss Goose, down at the brook, battling the clothes with her battling-stick," said Brer Rabbit.

Well, when Brer Fox heard that old Miss Goose was down at the brook dabbling in soap-suds and washing clothes, he took a peep at her. And when he saw how fat and sleek she was he licked his lips.

"One of these days I'll go and pay a visit to old Miss Goose and ask her how she's feeling!" said Brer Fox.

As soon as Brer Rabbit heard Brer Fox say that, he guessed there was something up. Brer Rabbit winked to himself, and thought he'd have some fun whilst he could. Soon Brer Fox said he must be going, so they said good-bye and went off.

Brer Fox set out for his home, but Brer Rabbit he slipped round and called on Miss Goose. She was down at the brook, washing and boiling and battling clothes.

Brer Rabbit marched up to her.

"Howdy, Miss Goose," he said.

"Howdy, Brer Rabbit," said Miss Goose. "I'd shake hands with you, but I'm all soapy."

"Don't worry about that," said Brer Rabbit.

Well, after Brer Rabbit had talked to Miss Goose for some time she told him she wasn't feeling very well.

"I'm getting stiff and I'm getting clumsy," she said, "and, more than that, I'm getting blind. Just before you happened to come along, Brer Rabbit, I dropped my spectacles into the washing-tub here, and if you'd come along then, Brer Rabbit, I might have thought you were that nasty sly Brer Fox, and I would have picked up my tub and emptied all the boiling suds over you! Yes, and you would have been properly scalded. It's a good thing for you I found my spectacles," said old Miss Goose.

"Well, now that you mention Brer Fox's name, I've got something to tell you about him," said Brer Rabbit. "He's a-coming to call on you, Miss Goose. He's coming, for sure—and when he comes, it will be in the night, Miss Goose!"

Miss Goose wiped her hands on her apron, and put her spectacles up on her forehead, and looked as scared as could be.

"Lawks-a-mussy!" said poor Miss Goose. "Supposing he comes, Brer Rabbit! What shall I do? There's nobody in the house but me!"

Then Brer Rabbit sort of winked at Miss Goose and said: "Miss Goose, the time has come when you must roost up high at night. If you don't roost up high, Sis Goose, Brer Fox will get you."

"What shall I do, what shall I do!" said poor Miss Goose.

"Now you just listen to me," said Brer Rabbit. "You go home tonight with your washing. Tie up a big bundle of clothes and put them into your bed. But don't you get into bed, Sis Goose—no, you fly up high on a rafter in the ceiling and roost there. And when Brer Fox comes, you let him grab the bundle of clothes on the bed and run off with them! You'll be safe, Sis Goose, so don't you worry any more!"

Well, Miss Goose said she was much obliged to Brer Rabbit, and she picked up all her things, and waddled off home, looking mighty scared. When she got home she did just as Brer Rabbit had told her to. She tied up a big bundle of white clothes and set them right in the middle of her bed. Then she sent a messenger to Mr. Dog and asked him if he'd mind coming round that night as she was feeling a bit scared.

So Mr. Dog, he came round and sat up with Miss Goose, and when she flew up to the rafter to roost he went out and lay down under the house.

Just before day, whilst it was still dark, Brer Fox came creeping along. He pushed on the door and it opened easily. He peeped in and he saw something big and white lying in the middle of the bed. He rushed in, grabbed the big white bundle, which he thought was Miss Goose, and off he ran!

Just then Mr. Dog rushed out from under the house, and if Brer Fox hadn't dropped the bundle of clothes he would have been caught.

Well, from that night the tale went round that Brer Fox had been up to Miss Goose's, stealing her clothes, and for a long time nobody asked Brer Fox out, and nobody said howdy to him when they met him.

Brer Fox thought that Brer Rabbit had told Mr. Dog to hide under Miss Goose's house, and bad feelings began between Brer Fox and Mr. Dog from that day. They hate one another even now, and as soon as Mr. Dog smells Brer Fox, and Brer Fox smells Mr. Dog, there's a great upset and they go scampering over half the country before they've finished with one another!

Brer Rabbit and Cousin Wildcat

Now Cousin Wildcat had not forgotten how Brer Rabbit had tried to set Brer Fox on him, and he lay in wait for him. And as Brer Rabbit was going along down the road, lickety-clickety, clickety-lickety, he suddenly felt something drop down on him! When Brer Rabbit pulled himself together he found that it was Mr. Wildcat hugging him from behind and whispering in his ear!

Old Mr. Wildcat had been lying stretched out on a tree branch that overhung the road, and when he had heard Brer Rabbit lickety-clicketing down the road he grinned to himself, and got ready to drop right down on him. And there he was, hugging and squeezing Brer Rabbit for all he was worth.

Brer Rabbit kicked and squalled. By and by he got his breath and said, "Oh! Oh, my goodness gracious me! What's happened now?"

Cousin Wildcat, he rubbed his wet nose on Brer Rabbit's ear, and made a cold chill run up his back. By and by he said, "Oh, Brer Rabbit, don't I just love you! You've been tricking all my cousins and my family, and it isn't so mighty long since you set Brer Fox on me so that I nearly tore him in two! Oh, Brer Rabbit, don't I just love you!"

Then Cousin Wildcat laughed and struck his teeth together close to Brer Rabbit's ear. Brer Rabbit spoke up.

"Goodness, Cousin Wildcat, the only reason I sent Brer Fox up to you that day was because I thought maybe you'd like to have him for your supper. Dear me, Cousin Wildcat, if you're going to be upset with me because of a thing like that, I'm not going to be friends with you any more!"

Mr. Wildcat wiped his nose on Brer Rabbit's ear, and looked

as if he were thinking hard. Brer Rabbit went on talking.

"Now just you tell me, Mr. Wildcat—have I ever bothered you? Just you tell me that!"

"No, Brer Rabbit, I can't say that you have bothered me," said Cousin Wildcat.

"No, you can't," said Brer Rabbit. "And more than that, Cousin Wildcat, I've done my level best to help you. And though you've jumped down on me like this and scared me dreadfully, I'm willing to do you another good turn to show you what a good friend I can be to you. I can hear some wild turkeys yelping out yonder, and if you'll let me off this time, I'll go out and call them up, and you can lie down as if you were dead, and they'll all come round you and stretch their necks out over you to see you, and you can jump up and get the whole lot of them before they can get out of the way!"

Mr. Wildcat listened and thought hard. If there was one kind of meat he liked better than another, it was turkey meat!

"Are you joking, Brer Rabbit?" he asked.

"Well, if I was off home walking by myself I might be joking," said Brer Rabbit, "but how in the name of goodness can I joke when you're on top of me hugging me so tightly, Cousin Wildcat?"

"Well, if you mean what you say, you can get up and call those turkeys here," said Cousin Wildcat, and he got off Brer Rabbit's back.

Wasn't Brer Rabbit pleased to get rid of him? He went into the bushes and began to yelp like a wild turkey, and he knew mighty well how to do that. Cousin Wildcat lay down on the ground for all the world as if he were dead.

Well, it didn't take Brer Rabbit long to get some turkeys along, for he was a good yelper, and all the turkeys came up to see who it was yelping. There they all came, with Brer Gibley Gobbler leading them. Brer Rabbit ran to meet them, and he winked at them, and whispered about old Mr. Wildcat, and how he was only pretending to be dead.

Well, by the time the turkeys got up to Mr. Wildcat, there was a great chattering and disputing going on among them. One turkey said Mr. Wildcat was dead. Another said he wasn't. Another said it looked as if he was. Another said it looked as if he wasn't. They stretched out their necks and lifted their feet high as if they were going to lean over Mr. Wildcat, but not one of them got too close to him!

Cousin Wildcat lay there and he didn't move. The wind ruffled up his fur, but he didn't move; the sun shone down hotly on him, but he didn't move. The turkeys gobbled and yelped round him, but they didn't go any nearer. They shouted and quarrelled about Mr. Wildcat, they stretched out their necks and lifted up their feet—but not a turkey went really near to Mr. Wildcat.

Well, they went on like this, enjoying the joke, till by and by Mr. Wildcat got tired of waiting and he jumped up, he did, and made a dash at the nearest turkey. But the turkey was ready, and when Mr. Wildcat ran at him he just rose up into the air, and Mr. Wildcat ran under him!

Then Mr. Wildcat ran at the next turkey, and that one flew up too. And it went on like this till poor Mr. Wildcat was so stiff in the joints and so out of breath that he just had to lie down on the ground and rest. And whilst he did this, Brer Gibley Gobbler and all his family flew on their way, laughing and yelping loudly.

When he got back his breath Cousin Wildcat looked round for Brer Rabbit. But he was nowhere to be seen. Cousin Wildcat shouted for him.

"Brer Rabbit! Hey, Brer Rabbit! Come along here. I want to talk to you."

But Brer Rabbit didn't come. So Cousin Wildcat got up and hunted round for him and he wasn't anywhere to be seen. Whilst all the gobbling and yelping had been going on Brer Rabbit had bowed his good-byes to every one and then run off as if a hundred dogs were after him! He wasn't staying till the end!

And the next day old Brer Gibley Gobbler sent him a fine turkey wing to make a fan out of, and Brer Rabbit sent it to Miss Meadows and the girls. My, what a fuss they made of Brer Rabbit for sending them such a beautiful present! He just sat there like a king and grinned away at everybody!

Brer Bear and Brer Bull-Frog

BRER BEAR WAS very angry because he hadn't caught Brer Rabbit after the trick he had played him in Brer Fox's pea-patch. He sat and thought how Brer Bull-Frog had told him where to find Brer Rabbit, and he was in a rage with Brer Bull-Frog because he had told him wrong.

He didn't know that what he had thought was Brer Bull-Frog was really Brer Rabbit sitting in a mud-hole, with only his big eyes sticking out, so that he looked like a frog! No—he thought it was Brer Bull-Frog all right, did Brer Bear.

"I'll pay old Brer Bull-Frog out if it takes me a year to do it!" said Brer Bear to himself. But he didn't have to wait a year, nor even a month, because hardly a week afterwards when Brer Bear was going home after hunting for honey in a bee-tree, who should he see but Brer Bull-Frog sitting out on the edge of a mud-puddle, fast asleep!

Brer dropped his axe, he did, and crept up. He reached out with his paw, and scooped old Brer Bull-Frog up just so! He scooped him in and there he was!

When Brer Bear had got his claws well over Brer Bull-Frog, he sat down and talked to him.

"Howdy, Brer Bull-Frog, howdy! And how are your family? I hope they are well, Brer Bull-Frog, because this day you've got some business with me that will last you a mighty long time!"

Well, Brer Bull-Frog was so surprised and scared that he didn't know what to say. He didn't know what Brer Bear had against him, and he didn't say a word. But old Brer Bear kept on talking.

"You're the man that sent me the wrong way after Brer Rabbit the other day! Oh yes, you are! You tricked me properly,

Brer Bull-Frog. You had your fun, and now I'm going to have mine!"

Then Brer Bull-Frog began to get scared, he did, and he said: "What have I been doing, Brer Bear? How have I been tricking you?"

Then Brer Bear laughed till he shook, but he went on talking.

"Oh no, Brer Bull-Frog! You're not the man that stuck your head up out of the water and told me Brer Rabbit had just gone by! Oh no! You aren't the man! Sure you aren't! I guess you'll say that about that time you were at home with your family where you always are. Well, I don't know where you were, but I know where you are *now*, Brer Bull-Frog, and I'm a-going to punish you for tricking me about Brer Rabbit the other day. You won't trick any more folks along this road!"

Well, of course, poor Brer Bull-Frog didn't at all know what Brer Bear meant, for it hadn't been he who had tricked Brer Bear at all—but Brer Bull-Frog knew something would have to be done, and that mighty soon, because Brer Bear was looking more and more angry and was snappmg his jaws together in a way Brer Bull-Frog didn't like at all.

Then Brer Bull-Frog began to shout and squeal. "Oh, pray, Brer Bear! Let me off this time and I won't ever trick you again. Oh, mercy, Brer Bear! Do let me off this time, and I'll show you a tree in the woods where the bees have a nest full of honey! It's the fattest bee-tree you ever saw! Oh, pray, Brer Bear, let me off!"

But old Brer Bear went on snapping his jaws and looking fiercer than ever. Brer Bull-Frog croaked in fright and squealed: "Oh, pray, Brer Bear! I won't ever trick you again! Oh, mercy, Brer Bear! Let me off this time!"

But old Brer Bear wouldn't listen to him. He meant to get rid of Brer Bull-Frog, and he sat and thought how he was going to do it.

"I can't drown you," he said, "because you live in the water. I can't burn you because I haven't got a fire. Now what shall I do with you, Brer Bull-Frog?"

Then Brer Bull-Frog stopped his crying and boo-hooing and said: "If you've made up your mind to kill me, Brer Bear, carry me to that big flat rock out there on the edge of the mill-pond, where I can see my family, and, after I've seen them, you can take your axe and hit me."

This seemed quite a fair and sensible thing to Brer Bear, and he agreed. He picked up old Brer Bull-Frog by one of his behind legs, slung his axe on his shoulder, and off he went to the big flat rock on the edge of the mill-pond.

When he got there he put Brer Bull-Frog down on the rock, and Brer Bull-Frog sat up and looked round as if he were saying good-bye to his folks. Then Brer Bear took a long breath and picked up his axe. He spat on his hands, lifted up his axe, and brought it down on the rock—*pow!*

Aha! That was just what old Brer Bull-Frog was waiting for! He knew Brer would have to lift up his axe before he could hit him—and between the time that Brer Bear raised the axe and brought it down again old Brer Bull-Frog leapt up and dived down into the mill-pond—*kerblinkityblunk!*

Well, Brer Bear nearly split the rock in half and almost fell into the water himself, he hit so hard! When he looked down, he couldn't see Brer Bull-Frog anywhere at all—but very soon he heard a little song being sung, way out on the pond.

It was sung by old Brer Bull-Frog, who had swum up to the top of the water, a good way from Brer Bear, and he was singing loudly:

> *"Ingle-go-jang, my joy, my joy,*
> *Ingle-go jang, my joy!*
> *I'm right at home, my joy, my joy,*
> *Ingle-go-jang, my joy!"*

But it didn't bring any joy to Brer Bear! He threw his axe at Brer Bull-Frog, who at once dived down out of danger. And old Brer Bear went home, grunting and groaning, declaring that Brer Rabbit and Brer Bull-Frog between them had lost him the best axe he ever had. Poor old Brer Bear!

Brer Rabbit and the Greens

ONCE UPON A TIME Brer Fox and Brer Bear went to get some greens for dinner. Brer Fox put his into a bag and Brer Bear put his into a basket.

And just as they walked around the field to go home, who should they see sitting fast asleep, leaning against a cabbage, but old Brer Rabbit!

"Look!" said Brer Fox, putting down his bag and creeping up to Brer Rabbit. "We've got him this time, as sure as ninepence!"

Brer Rabbit snored just a little. He was very tired, for he had been fishing all night long and had caught nothing at all. His whiskers fluttered as he breathed, and Brer Fox grinned to himself. This was easy! To think of all the times cunning old Brer Rabbit had tricked him—and now he was here for the taking!

Brer Fox caught hold of Brer Rabbit by the scruff of the neck, and there he dangled in the air, a very frightened creature.

"What's this? What's this?" squealed Brer Rabbit.

"Nothing much," said Brer Fox, stuffing Brer Rabbit into his big coat-pocket and holding him there. "I've caught you at last, that's all, Brer Rabbit. You shouldn't go sleeping out in the sun like that for every one to see you!"

"Brer Fox, your pocket is too warm," said Brer Rabbit, scrambling round. "Let me out for a breath of air."

"You're going to stay there," said Brer Fox. He picked up his bag of greens, and together he and Brer Bear went homewards, grinning at each other to think how easily old Brer Rabbit had been caught at last.

"Brer Fox, Brer Fox, I'm smothering!" cried Brer Rabbit. "Let me get my head out of your pocket, do! Just my head, so that I can breathe."

"It's no good your talking and talking and asking and asking," said Brer Fox. "I've listened to you too much, Brer Rabbit, and this time I'm not paying any attention to what you say. You're going home in my pocket, and my, but I'll have a good dinner today!"

Brer Rabbit didn't say any more. He just sat and thought hard.

Soon Brer Fox came to his house and asked Brer Bear in to have a drink of his honey-syrup, a thing Brer Bear was very fond of. The two put down their bag and basket of greens and Brer Fox banged the door.

Suddenly Brer Rabbit jumped right out of Brer Fox's pocket and ran scurrying round the room.

"Run, run!" said Brer Fox, laughing. "The windows are shut, Brer Rabbit, and the door is shut too, and Brer Bear is standing in front in case you think of opening it! Run, Brer Rabbit, and hide yourself somewhere. I'll find you, there's no doubt about that!"

Brer Rabbit didn't say a word. He ran under the bed and found a mat there. He hid beneath it. Brer Fox peeped under the bed and laughed.

"Ho, Brer Rabbit, aren't you clever enough to find a better place than that?" he cried. "I can see you, humping up that mat of mine! I can see you."

Brer Rabbit said never a word. He stayed under the mat until he heard Brer Fox pouring out the honey-syrup, and then he wriggled out from the mat and went quietly to where Brer Fox's big slippers stood at the other side of the bed.

Brer Rabbit took the slippers to the mat and humped them underneath so that it looked for all the world as if Brer Rabbit was still hiding under the mat himself!

Brer Rabbit grinned a little grin. He crept quietly to where Brer Bear had put down his basket of greens, and when neither Brer Fox nor Brer Bear was looking his way, he squirmed into the basket between two big cabbages. And there he lay as still as one of the greens themselves!

Soon Brer Bear said he must be going. He picked up his basket of greens and put them on his shoulder.

"Well, see you tomorrow, Brer Fox," he said. "Thanks for the honey. Now, where's that rascal of a Brer Rabbit? Don't let him slip out when I open the door, or you'll lose your dinner!"

Brer Fox looked under the bed and saw the humped-up mat. "It's all right!" he said. " Brer Rabbit is still hiding under the bed! I can see where his back hunches up my mat!"

Brer Rabbit knew it was Brer Fox's own slippers hunching up the mat, and he grinned to himself in Brer Bear's basket of greens.

"Well, good-bye," said Brer Bear, opening the door. He went out and shut it. "Huh!" he said to himself. "Old Brer Fox has got Brer Rabbit at last. No doubt about that at all!"

He walked on home. Presently Brer Rabbit gave a deep groan in the basket. Brer Bear stopped, very startled. He looked all round. Nobody was about at all.

Brer Rabbit groaned again. "Ooohahooohah!"

"Gracious goodness!" said Brer Bear, alarmed. "Whatever's that? Who's there? Is anybody ill? Shall I fetch a doctor?"

"Oooohah!" groaned Brer Rabbit in the cabbages, thoroughly enjoying himself now.

"It sounds as if it's in my basket!" said Brer Bear, terrified. "Can it be the cabbages talking?"

"Ooooh-ah-OOOOOOOH!" said Brer Rabbit, with a louder, deeper groan than ever. "Put me dow-oo-ow-oo-wn!"

"It *is* those cabbages!" squealed poor Brer Bear, and he put his basket down with a bump. Brer Rabbit made two holes in a cabbage leaf and stuck his big eyes through them. Just as Brer Bear opened the lid he saw the eyes looking at him, and he gave a squeal and fled down the road.

"My cabbages have eyes!" he cried. "My cabbages are looking at me!"

Brer Rabbit hopped out of the greens and laughed till he cried. Then he ate half a cabbage, put the basket on his back, and went off home, whistling.

On his way he passed Brer Fox's house, and saw Brer Fox looking gloomily out of the window.

"Heyo, Brer Fox!" called Brer Rabbit. "Did you find me under the mat all right? I hope you enjoyed your dinner!"

And with that he galloped off with the greens, lippitty-clippitty—just in time too, for Brer Fox jumped clean through the window and nearly caught him by the tail!

Brer Rabbit Gets a House

ONE TIME A WHOLE lot of the animals made up their minds they would go shares in building a house. There was old Brer Bear and Brer Fox and Brer Wolf and Brer Raccoon and Brer Possum—everyone right down to old Brer Mink. There was a whole crowd of them, and they set to work to build a house in less than no time.

Brer Rabbit was there too, of course, but he said it made his head swim to climb up the scaffold and build like the others, and he said too that he always got sun-stroke if he worked in the sun— but he got a measure, and he stuck a pencil behind his ear, and he went round measuring and marking, measuring and marking. He always looked so busy that all the other creatures said to one another that Brer Rabbit was doing a mighty lot of work.

And folk going along the road said that Brer Rabbit was doing more work than anyone. But really Brer Rabbit wasn't doing anything much, and he might just as well have been lying by himself in the shade, fast asleep!

The other creatures really built the house, and my, it was a fine house too! It would have been a fine house in these days, let alone those days. It had an upstairs and a downstairs, and chimneys all round, and a room for each of the creatures that had helped to build it.

Well, Brer Rabbit picked out one of the upstairs rooms for himself. Then he went and got himself a gun and put it up in his room. After that he got himself a brass cannon, and he dragged it up to his room one day when not one of the others was about. And after that he got himself a tub full of dirty, soapy water, and this he took upstairs to his room too, when nobody else was looking!

Well, when they had all got the house fixed up nicely, and were sitting in the parlour after their supper, Brer Rabbit yawned and stretched himself as if he were tired.

"Well, folks," he said, "I believe I'll say good night to you and go up to my room."

"Good night, then, Brer Rabbit," said all of them. Brer Rabbit went out of the door and up the stairs. All the others were chatting and laughing away as happy as you please, delighted with their new house.

Well, no sooner was Brer Rabbit up in his room than he opened his door again and stuck his head out of it.

"When a big man like me wants to sit down, where shall he sit?" sang out Brer Rabbit.

Then all the other creatures laughed and shouted back: "If a big man like you can't sit in a chair he'd better sit down on the floor!"

"Watch out down there, then!" yelled old Brer Rabbit, "because I'm a-going to sit down!"

With that, BANG! He let off his gun! Well, this sort of astonished everyone, and they looked round at one another in alarm, thinking that Brer Rabbit was a mighty heavy sitter-down.

"What in the name of goodness was that!" said Brer Possum.

They listened and they listened, but they didn't hear anything more, and before long they had forgotten about it and were chattering gaily about all kinds of things.

By and by Brer Rabbit flung his door open upstairs again, and stuck his head out.

"Hie!" he sang out. "When a big man like me wants to sneeze, where's he going to sneeze?"

Then all the other creatures they laughed like anything and shouted back:

"If a big man like you wants to sneeze he can sneeze where he pleases!"

"Watch out down there, then!" yelled Brer Rabbit. "Because I'm going to sneeze right here!"

And with that, Brer Rabbit let off his cannon—*bulderum-m-m-m-m*! It made such a bang that all the windows shook and rattled, and the house shivered as if it was going to fall down, and old Brer Bear, he fell out of the rocking-chair—*kerblump!*

When the creatures got over their fright a bit and settled down again, they looked at one another.

"Brer Rabbit's got a mighty bad cold," said Brer Possum, in a scared sort of voice. "I believe I'll just step out for a while, till he's got rid of it."

"I'll come with you, Brer Possum," said Brer Mink, getting up. "If Brer Rabbit sneezes again like that I'm not a-going to get any sleep in the house tonight, that's sure!"

So off the two went, arm-in-arm, and didn't turn up again that night. The other creatures watched them go, but they said they were going to stay, no matter how bad a cold Brer Rabbit had. And after a while they began to talk and laugh just as usual. About then Brer Rabbit opened his door again, and stuck out his head.

"When a big man like me wants to wash his hands, whereabouts is he to throw the dirty water?"

The other creatures glared at Brer Rabbit, and yelled back angrily:

"Big man or little man, throw your water where you please!"

Then Brer Rabbit yelled out: "Watch out down there, then—here comes my water!"

And with that he tipped up the tub of dirty water, and it went slish-sloshing down the stairs! And when the other creatures heard it coming they jumped up like mad and rushed to the doors and the windows! Some of them went out at the back door, and some of them went out at the front. Brer Bear fell out of the window, and Brer Fox tried to climb up the chimney-place. Some went one way and some went another—but they all went sailing out!

As for Brer Rabbit, he stood at the top of the stairs, grinning—and then he just shut up the house and fastened all the windows. Then he went to bed, he did, and pulled the covers up to his ears, and slept as if he was at peace with all the world.

"If those other creatures get scared and run away from their own house, what business is it of mine?" said Brer Rabbit. "I'm not scared of anything!"

And he never spoke a truer word!

Mr. Lion and Brer Rabbit Go Hunting

NOW THE MORE Mr. Lion thought about how Brer Rabbit tricked every one, the cleverer he thought Brer Rabbit was. And it came into his head that if he could make a friend of old Brer Rabbit maybe he'd get on a lot better. So he set off and found Brer Rabbit's house.

"Brer Rabbit, will you come hunting with me?" shouted Mr. Lion, banging at the door.

"No, Mr. Lion. I'm afraid you'd do all the hunting and I'd do all the running!" shouted back Brer Rabbit.

"Brer Rabbit, you're mighty clever, and I couldn't catch you if I tried," said Mr. Lion. "I give you my word I want to be your friend. Come on, now, and go hunting with me."

Well, when Brer Rabbit heard Mr. Lion say he'd give him his word, he knew Mr. Lion was speaking the truth, for no one had ever known old Mr. Lion to break a promise. So Brer Rabbit hopped out of his house and joined Mr. Lion. They each had a gun, and off they went across the countryside to hunt for food.

When they saw plovers in the air Mr. Lion raised his gun and shot, bang-bang! But he always missed. Brer Rabbit, he raised his gun and shot, and he always hit what he was shooting at. But no sooner did the bird he shot fall down than Mr. Lion would cry:

"It's mine! It's mine! I killed it!"

Well, Mr. Lion was such a big fellow that Brer Rabbit was afraid of quarrelling with him, but he made up his mind to get even with him. They went on and they went on. Mr. Lion kept missing his shots and Brer Rabbit kept hitting everything, and Mr. Lion, he always said the kill was his.

They hunted all day long, and when night came they were such a long way from home that they had to camp out. So they found a stream, and when they came to it they cleared a space, built a fire on the bank, and cooked their supper.

After supper they sat up and told tales, and Brer Rabbit, he said what a mighty good hunter Mr. Lion was, and Mr. Lion, he leant back on his elbow and felt mighty biggitty. Then, when Brer Rabbit saw Mr. Lion getting sleepy, he said: "I'm a monstrous heavy snorer, Mr. Lion, when I fall asleep, and I hope and trust I shan't disturb you this night."

Mr. Lion threw back his mane out of his eyes and said: "I'm a monstrous heavy snorer myself, Brer Rabbit, and I'll feel mighty glad if I don't rouse you up in the night too."

"Well, Mr. Lion," said Brer Rabbit, "I wish you'd be so good as to show me how you snore just *before* you get to sleep."

Mr. Lion drew in his breath mighty hard and showed Brer Rabbit, "Grr-grr, grr-grr!"

"Thank you, Mr. Lion," said Brer Rabbit, "and now I wish you'd be so good as to show me how you snore when you're really *sound* asleep."

Well, Mr. Lion, he sucked in his breath and made a snoring noise—"Orr-phm, grrrr-rr! Orr-phm, grrr-rrr!" and it sounded just as if a house was falling down each time!

Brer Rabbit looked astonished. He rolled his eyes round and said: "I always heard tell you were a mighty big man, Mr. Lion, and you surely are!"

Mr. Lion looked pleased. Pretty soon he shut his eyes and began to nod. Then he lay down and stretched himself out, and it wasn't long before he had begun to snore like he snored when he wasn't quite asleep—"Grr-grr, grr-grr!"

Brer Rabbit, he lay there. He didn't say a word. He just kept his eye on the bag where Mr. Lion had put all the birds that Brer Rabbit had shot that day. He lay there with one ear up and both eyes open. By and by Mr. Lion began to snore like he did when he was sound asleep.

"Orr-phm, grrr-rr! Orr-phm, grrr-rr!" he went. When old Brer Rabbit heard this, he got up and sprinkled himself all over with cold ashes from the fire, and then he picked up a whole lot of hot coals and flung them on Mr. Lion. Mr. Lion, he jumped up, he did, and asked who did that, and Brer Rabbit, he lay there on the ground and kicked at his ears with his hind foot and shouted, "Ow! Ow! Ow!"

Mr. Lion saw the ashes all over Brer Rabbit and he thought some one had been along and flung the fire over both of them to burn them. He didn't know what to think. He looked all round but he didn't see any one. He dropped his head and listened but he didn't hear anything either. Then he lay down again and dropped off to sleep. After a while he began to snore as he had snored before—"Orr-phm, grrr-rr! Orrphm, grrr-rr!"

Then Brer Rabbit jumped up again and sprinkled some more cold ashes on himself and flung some burning coal on Mr. Lion. Mr. Lion jumped up at once and yelled:

"There it is again!"

Brer Rabbit was lying on the ground, kicking and squalling.

"Hey, Mr. Lion, you ought to be ashamed of yourself, trying to burn me up like this!"

"Brer Rabbit, I never did anything of the sort!" said Mr. Lion. Brer Rabbit looked very doubtful. Soon he put his nose into the air and sniffed.

"Phewee! I smell old rags a-burning!" he said.

Mr. Lion looked angry. "It isn't old rags, Brer Rabbit. It's my hair a-scorching!"

Well, they both looked all round, they did, but they didn't see any one at all. Brer Rabbit vowed he was going to keep awake and do some watching next time, because he said he meant to catch whoever it was playing pranks on them. With that Mr. Lion lay down again and it wasn't long before he dropped off to sleep.

Well, then, the very same thing happened again. The cold ashes fell on Brer Rabbit and the hot coals fell on Mr. Lion! But by the time Mr. Lion jumped up Brer Rabbit was on his feet, shouting and pointing: "I saw him, Mr. Lion! I saw him! He's gone across the stream! I saw him!"

With that Mr. Lion let out a bellow and jumped right across the stream. He tore off, hoping to catch whoever it was that had thrown the hot coals on him, but he couldn't see any one at all, though he ran for miles.

And no sooner was he over the stream than old Brer Rabbit, he took up the bag of birds and shot off home lippitty-clippitty, as fast as he could! My, how he laughed to himself as he went, thinking what Mr. Lion would say when he got back to the camp-fire and found nobody there!

And what *did* Mr. Lion say? Well, when he found Brer Rabbit gone and the bag of birds gone, he just pawed up the ground and bellowed loud enough to be heard for ten miles round. All the creatures that heard him shivered in their shoes—except old Brer Rabbit, and it would take a lot more than that to make *him* shiver, wouldn't it!

Brer Fox Catches Mr. Horse

ONCE BRER RABBIT got Brer Fox into worse trouble than ever before. It was after Brer Fox had nearly got caught by Mr. Dog, and was lying in his house, snapping his jaws whenever he thought of Brer Rabbit, and wondering how he could trick him and pay him out for all the things he had done to Brer Fox.

Brer Rabbit got to hear that Brer Fox was planning how to trick him, and he thought it would be a good thing if he could get the better of Brer Fox first. Then old Brer Fox would lie low for a bit and leave Brer Rabbit alone.

Well, one day, when Brer Rabbit was going along the road, he saw a great big horse lying stretched out flat on its side in a field. Brer Rabbit crept up as near as he dared to see if the horse was alive or dead.

The horse lay quite still. Brer Rabbit crept up nearer and nearer, and by and by he saw the horse switch its tail, and then Brer Rabbit knew it was alive.

With that Brer Rabbit loped off down the road, and almost the first one he met was Brer Fox. Brer Rabbit shouted to him:

"Brer Fox! Oh, Brer Fox! Come here! I've got some good news for you! Come here, Brer Fox!"

Well, Brer Fox stopped, and when he saw that it was Brer Rabbit calling him he came galloping back, because it seemed as good a time as any to grab Brer Rabbit and take him home for dinner. But before he got too near, Brer Rabbit shouted again:

"Come on, Brer Fox! I've found a place where you can get fresh meat to last you till Christmas!"

"Whereabouts?" said Brer Fox.

"Just there in the field," said Brer Rabbit.

"What sort of meat is it?" said Brer Fox.

"It's a whole horse lying down flat on the ground," said Brer Rabbit. "We can easily catch him and tie him."

"Well, come on then," said Brer Fox, and off they went.

When they got to the field, there was the horse, sure enough, stretched out in the sun, fast asleep. Brer Fox and Brer Rabbit looked at him and began to squabble about the best way to tie him up so that he couldn't get loose. One said one thing and the other said another thing.

Then at last Brer Rabbit said: "The best plan I know, Brer Fox, is for you to get down in the grass and let me tie you to the horse's tail, and then, when he tries to get up, you can hold him down easily. If I were as big and strong a man as you, Brer Fox, I'd let you tie *me* to the horse's tail, and I'd hold him down myself. But I'm sure *you* could hold him down all right, Brer Fox. But if you're afraid, we'll drop the idea and think of some other plan."

Well, Brer Fox didn't quite like the idea of being tied to the horse's tail, and yet he didn't want Brer Rabbit to think he was scared. He always liked to talk biggitty in front of Brer Rabbit. So at last he said he would be tied to the horse's tail.

Well, Brer Rabbit made Brer Fox kneel down in the grass and he tied him up tightly to the horse's tail. Then after Brer Fox was tied up hard and fast, Brer Rabbit stepped back, crossed his arms and grinned till his mouth reached his ears.

"If ever there was a horse caught, then we've caught this one!" he said. "It rather looks as if we've put a bridle on the wrong end, but I expect Brer Fox has got the strength to hold the horse all right!"

Then Brer Rabbit cut a long switch from the hedge and trimmed it up, and when it was ready, he stepped up and hit the horse a rap—*pow*! The horse woke up very suddenly, and was so surprised that he leapt right up in the air and landed on his four feet. When he did that, of course, there was old Brer Fox dangling in the air, hanging from the horse's tail!

Brer Rabbit darted out of the way, and shouted loudly.

"Hold him down, Brer Fox! Hold him down! I'll stand out here and see fair play! Hold him down, Brer Fox! Hold him down!"

Of course, when the horse felt Brer Fox hanging behind him on his tail he thought something strange was the matter, and he began to jump round and rear up and down, and poor Brer Fox was shaken about like a rag in the wind!

All the time Brer Rabbit jumped around and shouted and yelled. "Hold him down, Brer Fox! Hold him down! You've got him now, for sure! Get a tighter grip and hold him down!"

The horse was really scared, and couldn't think what it was that bumped against him at the back. So he jumped up in the air and humped up his back, and reared and bucked, and snorted and stamped. But still Brer Fox hung on, and still Brer Rabbit skipped around, yelling and shouting.

"Hold him down, Brer Fox! You've got him where he can't get you! Hold him down, Brer Fox!"

By and by, when Brer Fox got his breath, he yelled back at Brer Rabbit.

"How in the name of goodness can I hold this horse down unless I get my claws in the ground? Stop jumping about there, Brer Rabbit, and come and give me a hand."

But old Brer Rabbit, he stood back a little further and shouted still more loudly.

"Hold him down, Brer Fox! Hold him down! You've got him now, for sure! Hold him down!"

By and by the horse began to kick out with his hind legs, and he kicked poor old Brer Fox so hard that he squealed. And then he kicked Brer Fox again so hard that he kicked him loose and sent him whirling over and over in the air and then down on the ground—*kerblap*!

And still wicked Brer Rabbit kept jumping round and shouting at the top of his voice!

"Hold him down, Brer Fox! Hold him down!"

But Brer Fox didn't want any more to do with the horse. He crawled away home—and on the way it sort of came to him that once again Brer Rabbit had played a trick on him. And he snapped his jaws and looked round—but old Brer Rabbit, he had gone home, laughing and rolling on the ground every time he thought of Brer Fox hanging on to the horse's tail!

Brer Rabbit and the Pears

ONE DAY, when Brer Rabbit trotted through the wood, he happened to see a little pear tree that was hung with large pears. He stopped and had a look at it.

"Those pears will be ripe next week," he said to himself. "And I'll be the one to pick them! My, won't they be juicy and sweet!"

So, the next week, he trotted by that way again and, sure enough, the pears were as ripe as could be. But somebody was up the tree picking them!

It was Brer Bear. Brer Bear liked a nice juicy apple or pear, and he had had his eye on that tree for a long time. And there he was, up in the tree, picking away as fast as he could, putting the ripe yellow pears into his basket, and now and then popping one whole into his big mouth.

Now Brer Rabbit wasn't in Brer Bear's good books at all just then, for he had taken some honey from a bee-tree that Brer Bear had specially wanted for himself. So it was quite a shock to Brer Rabbit to see Brer Bear there. He guessed Brer Bear wouldn't give him any of those pears just now.

Brer Rabbit looked at the little pear tree. He didn't like to climb up it in case Brer Bear pushed him down. No, that wouldn't do at all. But how in the world was he going to get any pears for himself?

Brer Rabbit sat and thought. Brer Bear hadn't seen him yet. Brer Rabbit crept off and went to Brer Terrapin's house under the water. He called down to him.

"Heyo, Brer Terrapin! Are you in this morning?"

"Oh yes, I'm in all right," said Brer Terrapin, and he swam up to the top of the water. "How are you feeling, Brer Rabbit?"

"Mighty hungry, Brer Terrapin," said Brer Rabbit. "Mighty hungry. And I've got a plan to get some fine juicy pears, if you'll come along and help me."

Well, Brer Terrapin liked pears too, so he clambered out of the water, shook his feet, and they set off together. Brer Rabbit told Brer Terrapin his plan, and Brer Terrapin laughed till he nearly cracked his shell.

By and by they came up to the pear tree. Brer Bear was still up there, picking the pears. Brer Rabbit and Brer Terrapin sat down under the tree for all the world as if they didn't know any one was there at all.

"Well, Brer Terrapin," said Brer Rabbit in a loud voice, "how's yourself?"

"Not too good, Brer Rabbit, not too good," said Brer Terrapin. "You know, ever since that tiresome Brer Bear tried to pull my tail out, I've had the trimble-trembles."

"Oh, he's a bad fellow, Brer Bear is," said Brer Rabbit. "I'm no friend of his and he's no friend of mine."

Now Brer Bear, sitting up in the tree, was most astonished and annoyed to hear all this. He sat there quietly, listening with both his ears.

"He's mean and he's selfish," said Brer Terrapin loudly. "That's what he is. And I wish he could hear me say so."

Brer Rabbit stopped himself giggling. "He's greedy too," he said. "Do you know, if he finds a bee-tree, he never even offers me a sip of the honey there?"

Now this was a real story, for Brer Bear had often given Brer Rabbit a share of his honey. Brer Bear, he sat up in the tree boiling with rage, longing to get at Brer Rabbit and give him a good slap.

"He's a slow chap," said Brer Terrapin. "My, you call me slow, Brer Rabbit—but if I ran a race with Brer Bear I'd be at the winning-post before he was half-way there!"

"And he hasn't as many brains as a caterpillar," said Brer

Rabbit, enjoying himself. "My, Brer Terrapin, what would Brer Bear say if he heard us talking like this about him?"

"What would he *do*?" giggled Brer Terrapin.

"I guess he'd throw something at us," said Brer Rabbit. "Yes, I guess that's what he'd do. Throw something at us, hard, and hit us. Ho ho! it's a good thing he isn't here, and hasn't got anything to throw!"

Well, this was too much altogether for Brer Bear. He gave a fierce growl, picked a large pear and threw it down the tree.

"I *am* here!" he grunted loudly. "And I *have* got something to throw! Take that—and that!"

Brer Rabbit and Brer Terrapin jumped up as if they were too astonished for anything. Brer Rabbit saw the pear coming and neatly caught it. The other one smashed on Brer Terrapin's shell. Brer Terrapin put out his head and began to lick it off with great delight.

"Goodness! It's Brer Bear up the tree!" said Brer Rabbit, pretending to be most upset and surprised. "He's heard all we said! Brer Bear, Brer Bear, now just stop throwing things at us. You'll hurt us!"

"That's just what I mean to do, you nasty tale-telling creatures!" roared Brer Bear, feeling angrier and angrier. He took a pear from his basket and threw it straight at Brer Rabbit. "Take that! Huh, I'll teach you to sit under a tree and talk like that about me! I'm throwing *this* pear for your story-telling— and *this* for your meanness—and *this* for your unkindness!"

Thud, plop, plop! Down came the pears! Some of them Brer Rabbit caught, others smashed on the ground and Brer Terrapin gobbled them up. One rolled away and Brer Rabbit picked it up.

"Stop, Brer Bear, stop! You'll hurt us!" cried Brer Rabbit, knowing quite well that Brer Bear would go on all the more if he were begged to stop. And so Brer Bear did. He was in such a rage that he threw down every pear in his basket, and picked

every pear off the tree. Down they came, plop, plop, plop, and Brer Rabbit picked them up in glee.

At last there were no more pears left to throw. Brer Rabbit looked up and winked at Brer Bear.

"Well, you won't be wanting your basket now, will you?" he said. "So what about throwing that down too, Brer Bear? It would be mighty useful for me to carry these pears home!"

And then Brer Bear knew that it was all a trick to get his pears, and he growled in rage. He began to climb down the tree, grunting and growling, and Brer Rabbit knew it was about time to go.

"Come on, Brer Terrapin," he said. "We've been here long enough. We'll go home."

So off they went, the two of them—Brer Rabbit with his pockets crammed full of ripe pears, and Brer Terrapin with his shell dripping with pear juice. My, how they giggled when they thought of Brer Bear throwing down his pears! Wicked Brer Rabbit—whatever will he do next?

Brer Rabbit up the Chimney

ONE DAY, not long after Sis Cow had tried to catch him, Brer Rabbit thought he would drop in and see Miss Meadows and the girls, so he got out his looking-glass and made himself smart. Then he set out.

As he went cantering along the road who should he see but old Brer Terrapin—the same old sixpence! Brer Rabbit stopped and rapped on the roof of Brer Terrapin's house. Brer Terrapin always carried his house with him, rain or shine.

"Are you in, Brer Terrapin?" asked Brer Rabbit.

"Yes, I'm at home," said Brer Terrapin.

"Howdy then, Brer Terrapin," said Brer Rabbit.

"Howdy, Brer Rabbit," said Brer Terrapin.

"Where are you going, Brer Terrapin?" said Brer Rabbit.

"Nowhere, Brer Rabbit," said Brer Terrapin. "Just ambling along."

"I'm on my way to see Miss Meadows and the girls," said Brer Rabbit. "Why don't you come along with me, Brer Terrapin?"

"I don't care if I do," said Brer Terrapin. So they set out together. By and by they got to Miss Meadows' house and in they went.

When they got in, Brer Terrapin was so low on the ground that he couldn't see anyone. He wasn't high enough on a chair so Brer Rabbit picked him up and put him on the mantelpiece. Brer Terrapin sat back there, he did, just as proud as a peacock.

Of course they all began to talk of Brer Fox, and Miss Meadows and the girls laughed loudly when they remembered how Brer Rabbit had ridden Brer Fox and stuck the spurs in him. They made lots of fun and giggled and joked. Brer Rabbit sat in his chair, smoking his cigar. Then he cleared his throat and said:

"I'd have ridden Brer Fox over this morning, ladies, but I rode him so hard yesterday that he went lame in one of his front legs, and I expect I'll have to get rid of him."

"Well," said Brer Terrapin, "if you are going to sell him, Brer Rabbit, sell him somewhere out of this district, because he's been here too long already. Why, I met Brer Fox along the road only yesterday, and what do you think he said to me?"

"Tell us, Brer Terrapin," begged the girls.

"He shouted out, 'Heyo, Smelly Shellyback!'" said Brer Terrapin.

"Oh my! Fancy that!" said Miss Meadows. "Brer Fox called Brer Terrapin a Smelly Shelly. How *could* he talk that way to a nice fellow like Brer Terrapin?"

But goodness gracious! Whilst all this was going on, Brer Fox was standing at the back door with one ear at the keyhole, listening! Listeners don't hear any good of themselves, and Brer Fox didn't either!

By and by Brer Fox stuck his head in at the door and shouted, "Good evening, folks, I wish you mighty well!"

And with that he made a dash at Brer Rabbit. Miss Meadows and the girls began to shout and squeal, and Brer Terrapin began to scramble round on the mantelpiece, and suddenly off he fell, and blip! He hit Brer Fox right on the back of his head!

This kind of stunned Brer Fox and he fell down on the floor. When he sat up again all he saw was a saucepan of greens overturned in the fireplace and a broken chair. Brer Rabbit was gone, Brer Terrapin was gone, and Miss Meadows and the girls were gone!

Brer Rabbit had shot up the chimney—and had knocked over the pot of greens in the fireplace. Brer Terrapin had crept under the bed and got behind the clothes-chest, and Miss Meadows and the girls had all run out into the yard.

Brer Fox felt the back of his head, where Brer Terrapin had dropped on him, and looked all round. But he couldn't see any sign of Brer Rabbit.

Soon the smoke and the ashes flying up the chimney got into Brer Rabbit's nose, and he sneezed—*huckychow*!

"Aha!" said Brer Fox, "you're up there, are you? Well, I'm

going to smoke you out, if it takes me a month. You're mine this time, Brer Rabbit."

Brer Rabbit didn't say a word.

"Aren't you coming down?" said Brer Fox. Brer Rabbit still said nothing.

Then Brer Fox went out to fetch some wood to put on the fire, and when he came back he heard Brer Rabbit laughing.

"What are you laughing at, Brer Rabbit?" said Brer Fox.

"Can't tell you, Brer Fox," said Brer Rabbit.

"You'd *better* tell me," said Brer Fox. "I'm just a-going to slam some wood on the fire, and you'll be roasted up there."

"Well, I'll tell you, Brer Fox," said Brer Rabbit. "I'm laughing because somebody's gone and hidden a box of money up here in the chimney, and it's right under my nose!"

"I don't believe you!" said Brer Fox

"Look up and see," said Brer Rabbit. So Brer Fox poked his head up the chimney to see, and Brer Rabbit kicked out with his feet and sent a whole heap of soot down into Brer Fox's eyes! Brer Fox rushed out to the yard to bathe his eyes, and Brer Rabbit came down from the chimney and said good-bye to the ladies.

"How did you send Brer Fox off?" said Miss Meadows, in surprise. "He came rushing out as if the dogs were after him!"

"Oh, I just told Brer Fox that if he didn't go along home and stop playing his pranks on folks, I'd take him out and whip him," said Brer Rabbit, twirling his whiskers.

And off he went, whistling as gaily as a blackbird!

Brer Fox's Fish-Trap

ONE YEAR THERE WAS a very dry summer, and the rivers and ponds got dried up so that there was hardly any drinking-water to be found. Even the big river got low, and as for the streams, some of them disappeared altogether.

The animals all had to go to the big river to drink. They met there, and the biggest ones drank first, and they drank so much that there was hardly any left for the little ones.

Brer Rabbit didn't mind very much. He always knew how to look after himself, and if any one was going to get water it was old Brer Rabbit. The other creatures saw his footprints by the riverside and they waited for him, but they never caught him.

Brer Fox wasn't so lucky. He always seemed to go for a drink when Mr. Lion and Brer Bull and the big creatures were there, and they crowded him out and chased him away. So poor Brer Fox, he was always thirsty and he didn't know what to do about it.

"I'll go along to Brer Rabbit's house and see how he manages to get a drink," said Brer Fox to himself, and off he set.

Brer Rabbit was at home. He was sitting outside his front door singing a little song:

> *"Oh, Mr. Rabbit, your eye's mighty big!*
> *Yes, sir, yes! It's made for me to see!*
> *Oh, Mr. Rabbit, your tail's mighty short,*
> *Yes, sir, yes! But it just fits me!"*

"Howdy, Brer Rabbit?" said Brer Fox.

"Howdy, Brer Fox?" said Brer Rabbit. "What are you wanting this morning? You look mighty down in the mouth."

"Brer Rabbit, I can't seem to get anything to drink," said Brer Fox. "When I go to the big river Mr. Lion roars at me, and Brer Bull crowds me out, and the rest of them chase me away. Now, you're a smart fellow, Brer Rabbit—can't you tell me how to get a drink when I want one?"

Well, Brer Rabbit, he sat and thought hard for a few minutes, then he grinned. "Oh yes, Brer Fox," he said, "I can tell you what to do. You've come to the right man for help, you have."

"What shall I do then, Brer Rabbit?" asked Brer Fox.

"You go home and rub some treacle over yourself," said Brer Rabbit. "Then go out into the woods and roll over and over in some leaves. They will stick to the treacle, and you'll be covered from head to foot with them."

"What shall I do after that?" asked Brer Fox, in astonishment.

"Well, you go down to the river and hide in a bush," said Brer Rabbit. "And when the creatures all come to get a drink, you jump out at them, Brer Fox—and you'll scare them all into the middle of next week!"

"Huh!" said Brer Fox. "That sounds mighty good to me, Brer Rabbit. I always said you were a smart fellow!"

"I haven't finished yet," said Brer Rabbit, who was really enjoying himself. "After you've scared every one away, go and wallow in the water and drink all you like—and pretty soon, Brer Fox, the fishes will all come swimming up to get a bite of treacle, and you'll be able to catch as many as you want to. And, if you're a nice fellow, Brer Fox, I'll take it kindly of you if you'll bring me one of the fish for myself."

"I'll do that, Brer Rabbit," promised Brer Fox. "Yes, I'll surely do that."

With that off he ran home. He went to his cupboard and took down a jar of treacle. He smeared it all over himself from head to foot—and a mighty sticky mess he looked when he had

finished! Then he went out into the woods and rolled over and over in the leaves and rubbish there till he looked as queer as could be!

When Brer Fox was ready he went down to the river and hid himself. By and by all the creatures came along to drink the water, and whilst they were a-pushing and a-scuffling and a-snuffling, Brer Fox, he jumped out of the bushes at them, and switched himself round and round, squealing loudly.

Well, all the creatures looked at this queer thing and they didn't know what to make of it at all! Brer Wolf saw him first and he was so startled that he jumped right over Brer Bear's head to get away! Brer Bear shot backwards, yelling, "Who's that? Who's that?"

Then every one saw the queer-looking creature and rushed away like apples rolling downhill, and before Brer Fox had time to do a few more squeals he had the river to himself!

The creatures didn't go very far. They soon stopped and looked round. Then they began to creep back a little nearer, trying to make out what this fearsome-looking thing was that had given them such a fright. When they got near enough to see, there was Brer Fox walking up and down, up and down, switching his tail about and squealing whenever he thought about it.

The animals didn't know what to think at all. They watched, and Brer Fox marched up and down. Still they watched and still he marched up and down. It went on like this till Brer Fox thought it was about time he made himself into a fish-trap and wallowed in the water as Brer Rabbit had said. Then the fishes would come up to him for a bite of treacle and he'd get an armful of them.

So Brer Fox marched into the water and lay down in it. He rolled over and over and wallowed in it, watching for the fishes to come. But they didn't come and they didn't come.

Brer Fox didn't know what Brer Rabbit knew! Brer Rabbit knew that as soon as Brer Fox went into the water the river would wash away the leaves and the dirt and the treacle—and there would be Brer Fox, plain for any one to see!

Well, the water washed away the treacle, and off went the leaves and the dirt downstream, and there was Brer Fox, just himself and nobody queer at all!

The animals were all watching Brer Fox rolling in the water—and bless gracious, how they stared when they saw the leaves floating off him and saw that he was just Brer Fox. Then they knew he had played a trick on them and they were mighty wild.

"Brer Wolf! Brer Wolf!" yelled Brer Bear. "You head him off down there, and I'll head him off up here. We'll catch Brer Fox sure as a fly's got wings!"

Brer Fox, rolling in the water, still watching for the fish that didn't come, heard Brer Bear's voice, and looked up to see what the fuss was about. When he saw Brer Bear coming one way and Brer Wolf coming another, he jumped out of the river in a mighty hurry. He took a look down at himself and saw that the treacle and leaves had gone—and then off he went as if a hive of bees were on his tail.

He wasn't any too soon. As it was, Brer Bear got the tip-end of his tail—another moment and he'd have caught him!

Brer Fox went home through the woods, wet and angry. As he passed Brer Rabbit's house he saw him out in the porch, rocking himself in a rocking-chair and singing his song:

> *"Oh, Mr. Rabbit, your ears are mighty long!*
> *Yes, sir, yes! My ears are made to last!*
> *Oh, Mr. Rabbit, your teeth are mighty sharp!*
> *Yes, sir, yes! They cut down the grass!"*

Brer Fox was going by without a word, but Brer Rabbit saw him. "Heyo, Brer Fox!" he shouted. "Have you brought me a fish from your fish-trap?"

But Brer Fox, he didn't answer a word. He gave Brer Rabbit one look, and if looks could have killed—well, Brer Rabbit would have dropped down dead, there isn't a doubt of that!

Brer Fox tries another Fish-Trap

NOW ALTHOUGH BRER FOX was very angry with Brer Rabbit for tricking him into making himself a fish-trap, he couldn't help thinking it certainly would be a mighty fine idea to make a real fish-trap. So he set to work to make one.

Brer Rabbit saw him working away at the trap and he walked over to see him.

"What are you making, Brer Fox?" he said.

"A fish-trap," said Brer Fox, rather proud of himself. "Why don't you make one too, Brer Rabbit? Fish is a change from fresh meat and salad."

"Thank you very much, Brer Fox," said Brer Rabbit politely, "but I'm not wanting fish for dinner just now, and anyway I'm too busy to make fish-traps."

Well, Brer Fox, he finished his fish-trap at last, and then he went in his boat up and down the river hunting for a good place to put it. He hunted and he hunted and at last he found the right place. He put his trap there and set it.

Then he rubbed his hands in delight and thought of all the fish he would catch. He didn't know that Brer Rabbit was sitting on the bank under a bush, watching him fix that trap. No—if Brer Fox had known that, he wouldn't have felt quite so happy.

Brer Rabbit watched Brer Fox carry stones and rocks to put on his trap to hold it in place. He grinned to see Brer Fox getting hotter and hotter.

Brer Fox felt very tired after all his hard work. He went home, washed his face and hands, and sat down to rest. After he had taken a good long rest he went down to the river to see if he had caught any fish in his trap. He was rather afraid of water-snakes when he put his hand in the trap, but all the same he felt all round the trap to see if he could feel any fish—and there were none there at all.

So back home he went once more. "I guess I must wait a few days before I go and look again," said Brer Fox. "I'll go down to my trap at the end of the week." So towards the week-end he went down to his trap, felt all round it, and was mighty disappointed to find no fish there.

It went on like this till Brer Fox was quite tired of running to and from his fish-trap and n

ver finding a thing there. And one day, when he was looking around his trap, he saw foot-prints that told him some one had been along there.

"Yes, some one's been robbing my fish-trap," said Brer Fox. "And if I don't make any mistake I sort of know who that some one is!"

He got into his boat, paddled it to an overhanging bush nearby and slid under it with his boat so that he was quite hidden. He watched all the morning. Nobody came. He watched all dinner-time and after, and nobody came. Towards the evening, just as Brer Fox was making ready to come out from under the bush and slip off home, he heard a noise by the fish-trap. He peeped out—and there was old Brer Rabbit in a boat, poling it along to the trap.

Brer Rabbit wasn't using a paddle to get his boat along, as Brer Fox did—no, he was standing up in his boat and using a long pole to push it along, just as we do when we are punting. Old Brer Rabbit, he stood in the back part of the boat, pushed his pole to the bottom of the river, gave it a shove, and sent his boat along at a good speed.

Brer Fox felt mighty mad when he saw this, and he watched and waited. "I'll just wait till Brer Rabbit comes by me and then I'll go after him in my boat and catch him!" said Brer Fox. "I guess I can paddle my boat quicker than he can pole his!"

Brer Rabbit poled right up to the fish-trap, bent down and put his paw into it. He pulled out a great big fish—then he reached in and pulled out another fish, then he pulled out a third, and it went on like this till he had got his boat almost full of fish from Brer Fox's fish-trap!

Just about then Brer Fox paddled his boat out from under his bush and came towards Brer Rabbit.

"Ah-yi, Brer Rabbit!" yelled Brer Fox. "You're the man that's been robbing my fish-trap all this time! I've got you this time! Oh, you needn't try to run! I've got you this time for sure!"

Brer Rabbit jumped round and saw Brer Fox. He flung the last fish into his boat, grabbed for his pole and started off, with Brer Fox just behind him. Now Brer Fox could paddle much faster than Brer Rabbit could pole, and Brer Rabbit knew this—but did he care? Not a bit of it! Old Brer Rabbit had a trick up his sleeve all right. He had more fun in getting away from Brer Fox that time than ever he had before in all his life!

How old Brer Bull-Frog laughed to see what happened! He was a-sitting there on the bank and he saw it all. Brer Rabbit had to stand at the back of his boat to pole it—and as soon as Brer Fox's boat touched his, Brer Rabbit took his pole and pushed hard at Brer Fox's boat. And the harder he pushed, the farther forward he sent himself and the farther backward went Brer Fox! Oh, it looked mighty easy to old Brer Bull-Frog sitting on the bank there, and all Brer Fox could do was to shake his fist and grit his teeth—but he couldn't get in front of Brer Rabbit's boat, no matter how he tried.

And when Brer Fox stopped to smack Brer Bull-Frog on the nose for laughing so much, Brer Rabbit slipped ahead, landed on the bank, took up the fish, and raced for home. Oh no, Brer Fox, you can't catch old Brer Rabbit!

Brer Rabbit Runs a Race

ONE DAY, when Brer Rabbit was going lippitty clippitty down the road, he met old Brer Terrapin, and after they had said how-do-you-do, Brer Rabbit told Brer Terrapin how grateful he was to him for falling off the mantel-piece on top of Brer Fox's head.

Then Brer Terrapin said: "Brer Fox ran mighty fast that day, but if *I'd* been after him, instead of you, Brer Rabbit, I'd have caught him."

"I could have caught him easily enough myself, only I didn't like to leave the ladies," said Brer Rabbit.

"I could have caught him before you did," said Brer Terrapin.

"You're an old slow-coach that doesn't start till other people have got there!" said Brer Rabbit.

"You mind what you're saying, Brer Rabbit," said Brer Terrapin. "I'm swifter than you, I am."

"I can outrun you any day, Brer Terrapin," said Brer Rabbit.

"I can be there and back before you've even started," said old Brer Terrapin.

"I tell you you don't know what you're talking about!" said Brer Rabbit.

"Well, in my chimney at home I've got a silver shilling hidden," said Brer Terrapin. "We'll have a race, Brer Rabbit, and if you win, then I will give you my silver shilling."

"And in my chimney *I've* got a silver shilling!" said Brer Rabbit. "And you shall have it if you can beat me in a race.

Huh, Brer Terrapin, I could leave you far behind, I could sow barley as I went along and it would be ripe before you got to the winning-post!"

Well, old Brer Turkey Buzzard said he would hold their shillings and arrange the race for them. Before long, everything was ready. The race was to be four miles, and the ground was measured off. At the end of every mile a post was stuck up.

"Brer Rabbit, you are to run down the high road, and Brer Terrapin, you are to run through the woods," said Brer Turkey Buzzard.

"Brer Terrapin is silly to run through the woods instead of down the high road," said Brer Fox. "He could get along more quickly on the road."

But Brer Terrapin stuck out that he would go through the woods. He had a mighty good reason for it too.

Miss Meadows and the girls and all the neighbours made up their minds to see the race, and Brer Rabbit practised for it every day, skipping over the ground as gaily as a grass-hopper!

Old Brer Terrapin lay low in the marsh. He had a wife and three children, had old Brer Terrapin, and they were all so alike that you couldn't tell one from the other. It was just impossible to know which was Brer Terrapin, which was his wife and which were his children.

Well, on the day of the race, Brer Terrapin, his old woman and his three children all got up before sunrise and went to the racing-place. Brer Terrapin's old woman took up her stand near by the first post, she did, and the children went one to each of the other four mile-posts, and old Brer Terrapin he took up his stand near the winning-post. So there was a terrapin by every mile-post.

By and by along came everybody to see the race. Judge Turkey Buzzard came, and Miss Meadows and the girls, and all the other creatures, and last of all Brer Rabbit with ribbons tied round his neck and on his ears. My, he did look smart!

Everybody went to the winning-post to see who was going to win, Brer Rabbit or Brer Terrapin. When the time came to start the race, old Brer Turkey Buzzard pulled out his watch and shouted out:

"Are you ready?"

Brer Rabbit yelled "Yes!" and old Mrs. Terrapin shouted "Yes!" from the woods. Brer Rabbit started out on the race and Mrs. Terrapin set off quietly for home. She hadn't got to do any more than shout "Yes!" to Brer Turkey Buzzard.

Judge Turkey Buzzard spread his wings and rose into the air. He skimmed along to see that the race was run fairly.

When Brer Rabbit got to the first mile-post one of the Terrapin children crawled out of the woods and made for the mile-post too. Judge Turkey Buzzard thought he was the same terrapin that had shouted "Yes!" to him at the other mile-post.

As Brer Rabbit reached the mile-post he yelled out: "Where are you, Brer Terrapin?"

"Here I come a-panting!" said the terrapin.

Brer Rabbit was surprised to find the terrapin so near him, and he set out faster than ever, and the terrapin made for home. He had no more to do in the race. But when Brer Rabbit reached the next mile-post, another terrapin crawled out of the woods near by. He was the second of the terrapin children, but he looked exactly like Old Man Terrapin himself.

"Where are you, Brer Terrapin?" shouted Brer Rabbit, as he got near the second mile-post.

"Here I come a-puffing!" said the terrapin.

Brer Rabbit set out again, faster than before, and came to the next mile-post—and there was the terrapin again. Brer Rabbit felt mighty surprised to think old Brer Terrapin could run so fast. He didn't know of the terrapin's little trick.

Then there was only one more mile to run. Brer Rabbit was getting out of breath.

By and by Old Man Terrapin, who was sitting in the woods not far from the winning-post, looked down the road, and saw old Brer Turkey Buzzard sailing along in the air, and he knew it was time for him to show up. So he scrambled out of the woods, rolled across the ditch and shuffled through the crowd of folks to the winning-post, and crawled behind it.

By and by along came Brer Rabbit. He looked round and didn't see Brer Terrapin. So he shouted out, "I've won the race, folks, I've won the race!"

Then Miss Meadows and the girls and everybody else began to laugh fit to kill themselves, and old Brer Terrapin, he raised himself up from behind the winning-post and said: "Just give me time to get my breath! I was here before you, Brer Rabbit, and I guess I've won the race and the money too!"

Then Brer Turkey Buzzard tied the purse of money round Brer Terrapin's neck, and, with everyone laughing and clapping, he ambled off home.

As for Brer Rabbit, he knew he had been tricked—but he just couldn't guess how, no matter how he kept on thinking!

Brer Rabbit Tricks Mr. Man

ONE DAY BRER RABBIT was going along the big road when he met Mr. Man driving along with a wagon full of greens. Mr. Man was taking them to market, and he meant to get a good price for them too!

Well, Brer Rabbit saw those greens, and he made up his mind that Mr. Man had too many, and he, Brer Rabbit, hadn't enough.

"There's something wrong somewhere," said Brer Rabbit. "If there wasn't, I'd have a wagon full of greens too! Now, why haven't I got one?"

When Mr. Man drove up, Brer Rabbit shouted to him:

"Mr. Man, please, sir, give me a lift!"

Mr. Man stopped his horse and said: "Heyo, Brer Rabbit! How's this? You are going one way and I'm going the other. What good is a lift going to do you when I'm going the wrong way?"

Brer Rabbit scratched the back of his neck with his hind foot and shouted out: "Mr. Man, you can't know me very well if you don't know I'll take a lift no matter which way I'm going!"

Well, after some time Mr. Man said Brer Rabbit could get up and have a lift.

"You come and sit here with me," said Mr. Man. "I'd like to talk to you to pass away the time."

"Oh no, Mr. Man," said Brer Rabbit. "I'd be scared of falling off if I sat in front with you. I'd rather sit right flat down in the bottom of the wagon."

So he climbed into the back of the wagon and crouched down there at the bottom as if he were afraid to move.

By and by, whilst they were going down a steep hill and Mr.

Man had to keep an eye on his horse, Brer Rabbit took hold of two big cabbages and flung them out on to the road. Just as they hit the ground with a thud, Brer Rabbit shouted out "OW!" at the top of his voice, to hide the noise.

Mr. Man looked round in surprise. "What's the matter?" he said.

"Oh, nothing at all, Mr. Man," said Brer Rabbit, "except that the wagon went over a stone and gave such a jolt that I nearly fell out."

Well, they went on a little farther, and Brer Rabbit took hold of two more cabbages. When Mr. Man had his eye on the horses Brer Rabbit threw the cabbages out—thud—on the road. Just as they hit the ground Brer Rabbit shouted out, "BLAM!" at the top of his voice.

This drowned the noise of the cabbages falling and made Mr. Man jump. "Whatever's the matter now?" he said.

"Nothing at all, Mr. Man," said Brer Rabbit, "except that I saw a big bird flying along and I pretended I had a gun and shot at him, blam!"

Mr. Man turned back to his horse again. Brer Rabbit waited until they came to a mighty slippery place and Mr. Man had to guide his horse carefully. Then he took up four cabbages and threw them out—thud! But just as they struck the ground Brer Rabbit gave such a loud yell that Mr. Man almost fell off his seat. "BLAM-BLAM!"

"Bless gracious, Brer Rabbit, whatever are you doing now?" yelled Mr. Man. "I nearly drove into a tree, you startled me so!"

"Sorry, Mr. Man," said Brer Rabbit. "I saw Cousin Wildcat making a face at me through the trees, and I just pretended I had a great big gun and shot at him, blam-blam!"

Well, Brer Rabbit kept on like this, making loud noises whenever he threw out the cabbages, till at last the wagon was quite empty. Mr. Man didn't notice this until he had got a good way to market, and then he looked round to say something to old Brer Rabbit—and saw that his wagon was empty!

Mr. Man stopped his horse and stared at the empty wagon in the greatest astonishment. "Where's my greens?" he yelled. "Where are my nice cabbages? Oh, you long-eared rascal! Where are my lovely cabbages? You give me those cabbages, Brer Rabbit, or you'll be sorry for yourself."

Brer Rabbit sat at the back of the wagon and listened as if he were mighty astonished. "Now, now, Mr. Man," he said, "just keep quiet. If folks come along this way they'll think you are acting mighty queer."

"You give me my cabbages, you long-eared scamp!" roared Mr. Man. "Look at all the way I've come to market to sell them—and now I'm nearly there and they've all gone!"

"Well, Mr. Man, I haven't got your cabbages," said Brer Rabbit. "That I haven't. Could I hide a hundred cabbages in my coat, do you think? No, that I couldn't. And I couldn't eat them all, either. No, Mr. Man, your cabbages have just disappeared, and it's no use asking me where they've gone, for I don't know where their friends are."

"You give me my cabbages," shouted Mr. Man, and he threw the reins on the horse's back and stood up to get hold of Brer Rabbit.

Well, Brer Rabbit began to get a bit scared and guessed it was time to go. So he dropped off the back of the wagon as nimbly as you please.

"The sun's getting low, Mr. Man, and I'd better be going. The sooner I go the better, because if you go on like this you'll soon be accusing me of taking all those cabbages, and you can see I haven't got a single one of them. Thank you for the lift, Mr. Man, and I wish you mighty well."

He trotted off down the road, carrying an old sack over his shoulder that he had found at the bottom of the wagon. And it wasn't long before that sack was full of cabbages—yes, as full as could be! Brer Rabbit picked up every one of them—and the only thing that surprises me is that he didn't get the horse and wagon as well! Oh, he's a sly fellow and a wicked one is Brer Rabbit!